Annabel's Starring Role

The *Triplets* Series

Becky's Terrible Term
Annabel's Perfect Party
Katie's Big Match
Becky's Problem Pet
Annabel's Starring Role
Katie's Secret Admirer
Becky's Dress Disaster

EMILY FEATHER

Emily Feather and the Enchanted Door
Emily Feather and the Secret Mirror
Emily Feather and the Chest of Charms
Emily Feather and the Starlit Staircase

Animal Magic

Catmagic, Dogmagic, Hamstermagic, Rabbitmagic,
Birdmagic, Ponymagic, Mousemagic

www.holly-webb.com

Triplets

Annabel's Starring Role

HOLLY WEBB

■SCHOLASTIC

Scholastic Children's Books
An imprint of Scholastic Ltd
Euston House, 24 Eversholt Street
London, NW1 1DB, UK
Registered office: Westfield Road, Southam, Warwickshire, CV47 0RA
SCHOLASTIC and associated logos are trademarks and/or registered trademarks of
Scholastic Inc.

First published in the UK by Scholastic Ltd, 2004
This edition published by Scholastic Ltd, 2014

ISBN 978 1407 14478 8

British Library Cataloguing-in-Publication Data.
A CIP catalogue record for this book is available from the British Library.

Printed and bound by CPI Group (UK) Ltd, Croydon, CR0 4YY
Papers used by Scholastic Children's Books are made from wood grown in
sustainable forests.

1 3 5 7 9 10 8 6 4 2

www.scholastic.co.uk

Chapter One

Annabel twirled and stretched, humming the music to herself, and critically watching her friend Saima, who was mirroring her moves.

"You're doing it wrong, Bel!" Saima complained.

"No, I'm not!"

"You did, you know," put in Katie lazily. She'd been lying on her bed reading a football magazine, and now she lifted her chin off her hands, and stared back at her sister.

Annabel shared a bedroom with her triplet sisters. It had originally been two rooms, and their parents had knocked it into one when they found out they were having three babies instead of just the one they'd been expecting.

1

It meant that even with three beds, and all her clothes, and Katie's sports equipment *and* a cage full of Becky's rats, there was just about enough room to choreograph a dance routine – if you didn't mind fitting it around the table where they were supposed to do their homework, Annabel sighed to herself.

She glared at Katie crossly, her hands in fists at her hips. She was pink in the face – they'd been dancing for at least twenty minutes *and* she was furious. How dared Katie say that? What did *she* know about dancing?

"Don't look at me like that! It's our bedroom, so if you're going to dance in it, you can't stop us watching. And you did do it wrong, I've seen the stupid thing four times now, and you missed out that twirly bit in the middle," Katie went on matter-of-factly.

"See!" put in Saima triumphantly.

Annabel scowled. Katie was extra-annoying when she was right. "I never liked that bit anyway," she said grumpily. "It looked silly.

There's no point doing babyish stuff – we want to look professional. I think there'll be loads of people from Year Eight and Nine at the audition, and we have to prove we're not just silly little Year Sevens. Do you want to end up as part of a chorus of *bunny* rabbits, or something like that?" she asked Saima threateningly, wagging a finger in front of her friend's face.

Saima grinned. "No, Bel," she answered obediently. She rolled her eyes at Becky over Annabel's shoulder as she turned away. Saima was very easy-going, and didn't mind Annabel being a bit overdramatic. It made her a lot of fun to be friends with – you couldn't be bored with Annabel around. Being friends with Annabel meant spending time with Katie and Becky too, which could be a bit weird sometimes. The triplets looked so alike (even when Annabel was wearing as much make-up as her mum would let her get away with and the others weren't wearing any) that everyone

3

thought they ought to like the same stuff and think the same about things. They didn't – and Annabel and Katie would get really cross if you mixed them up.

Saima glanced over at Becky, sitting on the window seat next to her rat cage, and cooing to Fang, her cinnamon-coloured rat, who was perched on the cage roof sniffing suspiciously at the piece of carrot that Becky had left for her. Becky wasn't as "look at me" as the other two. She was much quieter, and happy to hide behind Annabel and Katie quite a lot of the time. Annabel had confided to Saima that she was really shocked when Becky was the first of the triplets to start going out with someone. It was just a good thing that Becky's boyfriend David liked rats. Saima shuddered as Fang's little paws skittered through Becky's hair. She agreed with Annabel – rats were *not* something that ought to be in the house, certainly not in someone's bedroom.

"If we want proper parts in this play,"

continued Annabel grimly, "we need to be a lot better than the older ones, because Ms Loftus is automatically going to think Year Seven equals dancing bunny. Stupid teachers," she added bitterly.

"I didn't know that you had to dance at the audition anyway," said Becky, coming over, with Fang now cradled in both hands. "It didn't say so on the poster, just that you had to turn up straight after school on Tuesday."

"You have to be able to dance and sing if you want a main part," Saima explained, retreating slightly as the rat came uncomfortably close. "Ms Loftus said so. We asked her what the auditions would be like after Drama last week. We don't know exactly how she'll organize it, though – whether she'll get us all to do the same thing, or ask if we have anything we've already worked out."

"So we – need to – be prepared," gasped Annabel between high kicks. Then she stopped as she noticed where Becky was. "Hey! Becky!

This is the no rat zone. Out! You know the rules." She folded her arms and glared, and Becky backed meekly away.

"Sorry! I forgot, Bel, really."

Becky had agreed to Bel's rules for the rats because she knew it was the only way she could keep them, and because even though she couldn't understand *why* her sister disliked the rats so much, she knew that they really did make Annabel shudder.

"I suppose this isn't really the best place to dance." Annabel sighed. "Let's go downstairs where there's more room. We'll put the proper music on and you can see the whole thing!"

"Oooh yes, *let's*!" Katie muttered, but thankfully Annabel didn't hear her.

As soon as Annabel and Saima had disappeared out of the door, Becky grabbed the football magazine, and smacked Katie on the head with it. "Don't be so mean! She comes to watch your football games, even if she does spend the entire time moaning that she's freezing to death. She's really excited about this play, so you've got to be nice. Come on!"

Becky popped Fang back in the cage and took out her other rat, Cassie, before following the others downstairs. She had let Katie and Annabel name the rats because they were going to have to share a room with them, and Cassie's black and white coat had made football-mad Katie think of Newcastle United. Fang had been Annabel's choice – as she had said, to her, rats were nasty, slinky things with wormy tails and too many teeth.

There was plenty of space in the living room, so Becky, Cassie and Katie curled up on the sofa to watch.

Saima and Annabel both took ballet classes, and they were very good dancers. Saima also did Indian dancing, which seemed to give her an added grace, but Katie, watching them get into their starting pose, decided that Annabel really did have something special. Of course, there was no way she'd ever *tell* Bel that — she reckoned her sister was big-headed enough already — but there was something about the confidence in her moves that made her fun to watch. She was arched over backwards holding Saima's hands, as Saima knelt on the floor. As the music started, Saima somehow managed to get up very smoothly and they kept holding hands, so that they made an arch as Annabel straightened up. Then they spun out and the real dance began. Becky and Katie watched open-mouthed. How long had the two of them been practising this? Now they had the right amount of space, the steps that had looked a bit silly and clumsy upstairs seemed to flow into each other naturally.

It was all going brilliantly, but then someone else decided to join in. Annabel and Saima were doing a complicated sequence that involved crossing each other as they went from one corner of the room to the opposite corner, when Annabel noticed in mid-twirl that somehow Pixie, the Ryans' small black cat, had appeared with split-second timing just where her foot was about to land. She yelped, and managed to insert a sort of half-jump. Pixie gave her an affronted look, sat down, and started to wash in a way that strongly suggested that this was *her* floor, and Annabel ought to get off it. Annabel, scowling, introduced a new step that didn't quite fit into the music, the "scooping that stupid cat out of the way" bend and grab. Unfortunately, Pixie was not in a mood to be twirled with. She arched her back, and plunged her claws into Annabel's favourite lilac jumper.

Becky and Katie were in hysterics by this point. Annabel's face when she'd first spotted Pixie practically underneath her feet was bad enough, but Annabel trying to remember her steps *and* remove the cat was just too much. Saima had been trying to keep going, but she was giggling so much that she was bent almost double.

Annabel sighed, and stopped. Pixie leapt to the floor and stalked off indignantly.

Katie managed to stop laughing long enough to say, "That was fantastic, Bel. Not sure they'll let you take Pixie to school, though."

"Funny," muttered Annabel crossly. "If she's spoilt this jumper I'm going to kill her and make a black fur hat. Honestly, you can't move in this house without something furry getting there first."

"It was a brilliant dance, though," said Becky, trying to make peace with her sister. "Wasn't it, Katie?" She raised her eyebrows at Katie, wanting her to be nice to Annabel, but Katie looked like she was still trying not to laugh.

Annabel sighed dramatically and began inspecting her jumper to make sure there really weren't any pulled threads. It was so unfair. The dance had been looking so good – they'd never got it as perfect as that before – and now it was all spoilt. They should have gone over to Saima's house, which was always beautifully tidy, with no dumb cats messing things up, and certainly no *rats*. She scowled.

Becky headed for the stairs. "Look, I'm really sorry about Pixie. If I go and put Cassie upstairs, and shut the cats out, will you do the dance again in a minute?" Then she glared at Katie – *back me up!*

Katie got the signal this time. "Please, Bel. It really was good, way better than it looked upstairs when you hadn't got the music. I want to see how you finish it. You don't mind doing it again, do you, Saima?"

"The end's the best bit, actually." Saima nodded enthusiastically.

Annabel looked pleased. She hadn't expected Katie and Becky to be so interested – after all, dancing was something neither of them were that keen on – but they seemed to really mean it. She bounced over to the CD player, her bad temper gone as quickly as it had arrived.

Becky popped her head back round the door. "Shall I get Mum, as well? I bet she'd like to see it."

Annabel shrugged, and tried to look as though she didn't mind either way. "OK," she said in a don't-care voice, secretly delighted at the fuss Katie and Becky were making.

The second performance was slightly less eventful. Katie and Becky and their mum clapped loudly at the end – they'd been going to anyway, to cheer Annabel up, but actually they did it without needing to think.

"I can't believe you two made that up!" enthused Mrs Ryan, as they sat round the kitchen table sharing a packet of chocolate biscuits. "It was wonderful. So this is for the Christmas play that the school's putting on at the end of term, is it? What parts do you two want?"

Annabel flushed slightly. She wasn't really sure how her family would react if she said she was after the main part – Cinderella. Annabel knew that she was a good dancer – she wasn't being conceited, she just *was*. And she adored acting. But was she good enough to take the lead role in a school play? It would be so cool! Obviously any part would be fun – as long as it wasn't a dancing bunny rabbit – but secretly she wanted to be the star. All this ran through her mind as she hesitated, wondering how to answer her mum's question. Then she shrugged, and grinned round at the others. Why not admit it? "The bigger the better."

"Well, why not," said Mrs Ryan. "You're certainly good enough, Bel."

Katie and Becky rolled their eyes at her, but Annabel felt encouraged. Saima and her sisters hadn't said she was aiming too high – it was as though they thought she might really be able to get a big part.

Saima nodded. "Me too. I'd like to do lots of dancing. And I want something with a nice costume!"

Katie rolled her eyes again. "Honestly. You two are obsessed with clothes!"

"Uh-huh." Saima nodded happily. "Oooh, Bel, talking of clothes, do you want to come Christmas shopping in Stallford with me soon? My uncle sent me some money to get my own present, and I want to get stuff for people at school too."

Annabel grinned smugly. "OK. But I probably won't need to get that much. We're doing most of our Christmas shopping in Oxford Street." She tried to say this in an offhand kind of way, but she couldn't hide the excitement in her voice.

Saima's perfectly arched eyebrows nearly disappeared into her hair. "You're going shopping in *London*?" she squeaked.

"Mmm. Our Auntie Janet lives there and we're going up to see the Christmas lights and do our present-shopping – isn't it cool?"

Saima looked hugely envious. "You're so lucky! You'd better get me something nice, Bel!"

Later on, when they'd walked Saima back home and Annabel was sitting on the stairs, supposedly finishing off her homework to hand in the next day, her brain wouldn't stick on maths (it hardly ever did). Instead she made a big decision. Mum, and Katie and Becky, and Saima all seemed to think she had a good chance at the auditions. So she was going to do whatever it took to get the main part – Annabel Ryan was going to be the star. . .

Chapter Two

Annabel couldn't believe that there were two whole days of school to get through before the auditions. How could she be expected to cope with stupid stuff like the periodic table and equilateral triangles, for heaven's sake? She was clearly not in the mood at all for school that Monday, and Katie cast an anxious eye over her as they walked across the school grounds on their way to the last lesson of the morning.

"Bel, you need to be sensible. It's French, and you know what Mr Hatton's like. He'll have a real go at you if you mess around with him like you were in science. Even Mrs Stafford was looking at you funny, and she never tells *anyone* off."

This was true. Mr Hatton was well known as a teacher that you didn't want to get on the wrong side of. He also appeared to be distinctly suspicious of the triplets, as if he was convinced they were plotting something all the time. Annabel had had a real run-in with him a few weeks earlier, when she'd entirely forgotten to learn her French vocab for a test, so normally Katie's warning would have sobered her up. Today, though, she just felt too buzzy and excited to care much, and only managed to calm down enough to give her sister a withering look.

"Stop *fussing*, Katie! You're so boring." She stalked ahead of Katie and the others into the classroom. Katie grimaced at Becky – this was typical Annabel. Then she sighed. Why did she feel like she was going to be mopping up the mess any minute?

It was unfortunate that the scramble for seats had left the triplets at a table right next to Max Cooper and his mates. Max was Public

Enemy Number One as far as they were concerned – on days when they managed to avoid blonde brat Amy Mannering, anyway. Max took every opportunity he could to get at the triplets. He especially had it in for Katie, as she'd got him into big trouble a while back after he deliberately injured her in a football match. Max's dad had gone ballistic at Max after Mrs Ryan phoned him to complain, and Max was still holding a grudge.

"Oh, great. It's the *triplets*. Ben, pass me your rucksack, I need something to be sick in."

Ben, who wasn't nearly as horrible as Max, snickered uneasily, and tried not to look nervous. Katie and Annabel were both well known for giving as good as they got.

"How's your leg, Katie? Awww, did you need Mummy to kiss it better?"

Katie was just drawing breath to blast Max with a detailed description of the close family relationship between him and a very backward slug when Annabel got in first.

"Shut up, bug-brain! Go on, be sick — at least it'll mean you're not talking."

At that moment Mr Hatton came in, and Annabel had the sense to turn round and look innocent — although her angelic expression only made the French teacher give her a suspicious look.

Max was obviously in the same devil-may-care mood as Annabel, because he spent the whole lesson hissing insults at her, and kicking her chair in the most irritating way. And somehow he managed it without Mr Hatton noticing. So when Annabel finally lost her temper literally two minutes before the end of the lesson — it was the fourth time Max had pulled her hair — and emptied her pencil sharpener over his head, Mr Hatton was not understanding. He had the good sense to put Max in detention, but he put Annabel in too — for Tuesday after school.

"But Mr Hatton, you can't — I—"

"Quiet!" Mr Hatton refused to listen. In

fact he threatened to give Annabel a detention every Tuesday for the rest of the term if she didn't shut up. So she shut up.

To make everything worse, as soon as the bell went Amy sauntered over with a gloating little smile. "Oh, Annabel! I can't believe he gave you a detention for tomorrow! You must be *so* disappointed. You and your sisters would definitely have got parts – I'm sure Ms Loftus could have rewritten Cinderella so that I had three Ugly Sisters." Amy paused, waiting for a comeback, but for once Annabel was too shocked to argue. Amy smiled perfectly and went to the door, purring over her shoulder, "Never mind, there's always next year. And don't worry, I'll explain to Ms Loftus that you couldn't make the audition."

Annabel watched blankly as Amy disappeared with a last maddening flick of strawberry-blonde hair. So much for Annabel the star. Not only was she going to miss the chance to try for Cinderella, it was clear that

Amy thought she was going to be the lead. Amy Mannering to get *her* part? It was unbearable.

Katie looked at Annabel's white face and bit back the I-told-you-so-type comment she was very tempted by. It was clear that Annabel didn't need telling. Becky put an arm round her sister, and wisely didn't even try saying something comforting. Saima looked rather lost – how could she go and audition without Annabel when they'd planned it all together?

Annabel stopped staring after Amy and looked round at them all. Her gaze settled on Katie, almost hopefully. The oldest of the triplets, she was often the one to sort things out for her sisters. But Katie didn't seem to be bursting with ideas – she just looked sympathetic and that was no use at all.

Becky looked back and forth between the two of them, unable to bear Annabel's defeated expression.

"Look, why don't we go and explain to Mr Hatton, and see if he'll change the day? I mean, if he understood. . ." Her voice petered out as she realized that everyone was staring at her as though she was mad. "Well, he might," she added defensively.

"Mr Hatton?" said Katie in a disbelieving voice, and Becky gave up.

The triplets moved round school in a depressed bunch for the rest of that day. Annabel was normally so sparkly and funny that when she was down it really affected the others.

They spent Monday evening desperately trying to think of something they could do. Annabel knew there was no point asking Mum to intervene. After she'd got into trouble with Mr Hatton the last time, and then a couple of other teachers had written sarcastic comments on her homework, Mum had had a serious talk with Bel about concentrating and being sensible. When they got home from school she had to give Mum the detention slip to sign, and she looked so disappointed that Annabel just wanted to cry. Mum had been so excited about her being in the play the day before, and now Annabel would have to explain that she'd missed the auditions. Oh, it just wasn't fair.

They had loads of Science homework that had to be in on Tuesday morning but Annabel was in no state to do it. Katie and Becky decided to fake her handwriting after realizing that she'd spent a whole hour sitting on the stairs (her homework spot) doing nothing except stare at the banisters. They dragged her upstairs, so that she at least had some company, and set about working out some Annabel-style mistakes.

On Tuesday Amy's gloating little smile made everything ten times worse for Annabel. Every time she turned round Amy seemed to be there – smiling. By last lesson that afternoon, Annabel was positively drooping – even her hair seemed to have lost some of its glossy silkiness. She hadn't had the energy to curl it that morning like she often did, and it was trailing across her shoulders, without any fancy clips even. She wandered gloomily out of the classroom after Becky and Katie and Saima and the others, her shoulders getting lower and lower as they walked down the corridor past the main hall. Lots of people from Years Seven, Eight and Nine were gathering excitedly outside the hall, and there was a buzz of nervous chatter filling the corridor as they waited for Ms Loftus. Katie looked apologetically back at Annabel. Going past the hall was the quickest route to the classroom where Annabel's detention was being held, but she wished she'd thought to take another route. Annabel actually flinched when she heard Amy's sharp laugh from the middle of the crowd.

But seeing Amy's knowing smile stopped Katie dead. She grabbed Annabel's arm and signalled fiercely to Becky and the others to follow her, then she shot off back up the corridor, dragging Annabel like a limp fish.

"What? What's going on?" Becky panted, as she caught up with Katie at one of the window alcoves back round the corner from the hall.

"I've got it! You can go to the audition, Bel! It just struck me as I saw that idiot Amy. There's no way I'm letting her be in that play when you can't!"

Annabel only managed a feeble lift of one eyebrow, but everyone else was more enthusiastic.

"What are you going to do?" squeaked Saima excitedly. She really hadn't been looking forward to auditioning without Annabel.

"Yes, what?" asked Megan, shrugging. "I mean, Annabel can't be in two places at once."

"Can't she?" Katie grinned evilly. "Why not?"

Megan, Saima and Fran looked blank, but

Becky jumped off the radiator where she'd been perched, and gave Katie a hug. "Of course! Katie, you're a genius. Isn't she, Bel?"

A little of Annabel's usual sparkle seemed to come back. "Would you really do it? You mean it?" she asked disbelievingly. "You could get into big trouble if you're caught. And so would I, I suppose."

"Caught doing *what*?" demanded Saima, looking back and forth between the triplets.

Katie grinned, and pulled off the band that was holding her hair in a tight knot at the back of her neck. Then she combed her hair out with her fingers, while Annabel fossicked through her bag for a brush and some lipgloss. Thirty seconds later, Saima and the others were beginning to get the idea. No one would be able to tell which one was which – especially after they swapped Annabel's green cardigan for Katie's sweatshirt.

"You're really going to owe me for this, Bel, just remember," Katie warned. "Go on – you need to get to the hall quick. We'll see you later. Break a leg!"

Annabel hugged her, and then raced back down the corridor, closely followed by Saima. Annabel the star was back!

Katie was feeling pretty nervous as she sat down in the classroom where Annabel's detention was being held. She really hoped she could pull this off, otherwise she and Bel were in big trouble. She'd just have to pray that neither Max nor Mr Jones suspected anything.

She looked down at her sheet of paper – she was supposed to be writing an essay on responsible behaviour, but it was difficult to concentrate. For a start, she could see Max over the other side of the room, and even the sight of him was annoying – and whenever he could catch her eye he pulled faces and mouthed insults at her. When the triplets' mum had phoned up Max's dad to complain about him injuring Katie, she'd got off the phone looking really sad, and told them they should try and be understanding to Max. His mum had died two years before, and he and his dad were on their own. That was all very well, Katie thought, and they did try and remember, but it didn't make him any less horrible. She scowled at Max as he stuck his tongue out at her *again*. Ha! Mr Jones, who was taking detention, had spotted him, and given him a freezing glare. Max studiously bent over his essay.

Katie managed another sentence – *I could have hurt somebody accidentally* – honestly, how on earth was she meant to get a whole sheet of paper out of this? She decided to write bigger. She was sure no one was going to read it, anyway. The only thing more boring than writing these stupid essays would be reading them, and Mr Jones looked as though he just wanted to go home.

The other problem was that Katie couldn't stop wondering how the audition was going.

She grinned to herself. Annabel's face when she'd realized what Katie was suggesting — she'd gone from dejected to glitter princess in about two seconds flat. Katie was sure she'd be brilliant; she just hoped that her sister would get the part she wanted. And that Amy wouldn't. . .

She came out of her daydream to find Mr Jones staring straight at her and looking cross. "Annabel! How many times do I need to ask you? Stop staring into space and get back to work, please."

Katie gaped at him, and then suddenly, nervously, remembered that she *was* supposed to be Annabel and started writing fast.

The real Annabel was onstage at that very moment, and loving it — especially because she could see Amy seething. As Annabel and Saima had dashed into the hall, Amy's face had fallen dramatically. She obviously couldn't understand how Annabel had escaped detention, and she just couldn't take her eyes off her. At the start of the auditions Ms Loftus had got them to read a bit of the play, swapping round parts until everyone had had a go, while she made loads of notes. Now they'd gone on to dancing. She'd explained that everyone in the play would need to sing and dance a bit (at which some of the boys looked decidedly less than keen) and main characters would have solos. Then she'd demonstrated a few steps that she wanted everyone to do, while Mr Becket, one of the music staff, played the piano. Annabel and Saima had looked at each other and grinned – the steps were so easy! The routine they'd been practising on Sunday was much more complicated. When Ms Loftus called for six volunteers to have a go, their hands shot up. Ms Loftus coaxed four more girls up onstage. Annabel and Saima muttered together while they waited for Ms Loftus to finish going through the steps once more for one of the other girls who'd suddenly gone into a fit of the jitters. Obviously they couldn't change the steps she'd asked them to do – she might think they'd just got them wrong – but surely they could add a little something? "We just need to do it perfectly," said Saima, shaking her head. "And maybe add some finishing touches. I mean, Ms Loftus is an OK dancer" – Saima said this with her head on one side, critically watching the Drama teacher's efforts – "but she's doing nothing with her hands, look. And her head position is just messy."

Annabel giggled. Saima sounded so like their ballet teacher, Mrs Flowers, it was uncanny. But she saw Saima's point. What they needed to do was take those rather boring steps and make them look like something really special.

So while the other girls went through the routine just about OK, with worried faces, and little rushes to catch up when they finally remembered what the next bit was, Annabel and Saima put on a real performance. Crisp turns, perfectly finished steps, and a general impression that although of course they were enjoying themselves, this was so easy it came as naturally as walking.

It worked. Ms Loftus smiled delightedly at them as they came offstage, and made furious notes on her pad. She wasn't the only one to have noticed. Amy was hissing nastily to her little cronies Cara and Emily: "Did you *see* them showing off like that? They're just so desperate, it's really sad."

Annabel and Saima exchanged grins as they sat down, and Annabel raised her eyebrows at Amy – as though she couldn't even be bothered to comment. It was easy to tell when Amy was rattled; that was when she started to be really nasty. And now there was a definite undertone of panic in her voice. Interesting that *she* hadn't volunteered to dance yet, thought Annabel. Hmmm. Maybe dancing wasn't Amy's strong point.

Suddenly Saima nudged Annabel. "Look," she muttered out of the side of her mouth. "Over there. Josh Matthews. He's smiling at you."

It was true. Annabel had been so excited about getting to audition after all that she hadn't even noticed Josh, but there he was, sitting with a group of Year Eights, including his girlfriend Julianne. Annabel sighed. Normally she was very happy with her appearance, but blonde hair and blue eyes weren't very, well, *exciting*, she decided sadly, envying Julianne's dark-red hair and green eyes. She smiled shyly back at Josh, and watched with interest as he volunteered to be in the next dance group, dragging Julianne and his mates up there with him.

It was cheering to know that even if Julianne was striking, she was a useless dancer. She was about two steps behind all the way through, and she looked terrified. Josh, on the other hand, was really good. *Huh*, thought

Annabel. *Gorgeous, funny, and a brilliant dancer. And taken. Not fair.*

Josh smiled at her again as he went to sit down. He was walking behind Julianne, and as he passed Annabel and Saima he rolled his eyes in her direction. Clearly he thought she was a useless dancer as well. Maybe Josh wasn't as taken as all that? Annabel mused. And then she mentally told herself off. Nicking other people's boyfriends was not something she wanted to get known for. But there was no harm in hoping that Josh just got sick of Julianne, was there. . .?

Chapter Three

Becky had walked home with Fran, and she was on tenterhooks waiting for the others to get back. Had it worked? Or had someone caught Katie out? She wandered round the house clutching the Ryans' ginger cat Orlando like a furry hot-water bottle, and clock-watching. She'd told Mum that Katie had an extra football practice – she felt awful lying to her, but the audition was so important to Annabel. If Katie could go as far as actually pretending to be her sister, then Becky could tell a tiny little lie to Mum, couldn't she? Luckily Annabel hadn't told their mum when the auditions were going to be, so Mum wouldn't realize she'd been in two places at once – she'd just assume the auditions had been in the lunch-hour or something. Finally she spotted Katie and Annabel coming down the road with Saima. Becky dumped Orlando unceremoniously on her bed and dashed downstairs and out of the front door.

"How did it go?" She didn't really need to ask – one look at Annabel's face was enough to show that she'd been having the time of her life.

"It was fantastic, it was brilliant – oh, Becky, it's so exciting!" Annabel threw her bag on the ground and hugged her sister, then grabbed Katie and Saima too, and dragged them dancing round in a massive moving hug.

"And no one noticed?" Becky asked Katie anxiously when Annabel finally let go.

"Nope, it was fine. I'm never doing that again, though, Bel. It was so boring – you can do your own detention next time."

The mood in the Ryans' house that night

was totally different to the night before. Annabel was jubilant. She didn't know yet what part she'd got in the play, but she did know that she had managed to show off to the best of her ability at the audition. After all, she reasoned, that's what auditions *were* – the ultimate opportunity to show off, without anyone having a go at you about it. Well, apart from Amy Mannering, and who cared about her?

Unfortunately, Amy was the very person that Annabel *should* have been worrying about. The following day she was still furious that Mr Hatton had apparently let Annabel off her detention – how else could she have been at the audition? At registration on Wednesday morning she was holding forth on this to Emily and Cara.

"It's just typical. Those triplets get away with everything – they just have to smile at the teachers and they get let off."

This was actually true, in a way, but Amy was cleverly leaving out the fact that the triplets were generally nice, and being nice got them a long way.

Cara and Emily nodded wisely – they tended to do this a lot round Amy, as she was the kind of person who just wanted people to agree with her.

"Mr Hatton's really strict with everyone else, so why should Annabel get away without a detention? We ought to *tell* someone."

Amy brooded silently on the injustice of all this for a minute or so, but then she got an unexpected interruption. Max had been listening to her complaining, and although he wasn't sure what was going on, he was one of those people with a sixth sense for stirring up trouble, especially if it involved one of the triplets. . .

"Did you say that Annabel Ryan was at that audition yesterday?" he asked Amy curiously.

Amy looked down her perfect little nose at

him. "Yes," she said, rather frostily. "Why do you care?"

Max's whole face seemed to sharpen up, like a dog getting on a scent. "Because she was in detention at the same time, you know. Or at least, *somebody* was."

Amy leaned forward eagerly. She wasn't stupid. "One of the other two did her detention for her?"

Max nodded. "It must have been Katie," he said thoughtfully. "Becky wouldn't do it, I don't reckon. She's too wimpy."

They grinned at each other delightedly, practically rubbing their hands. The triplets were going to be in so much trouble! They were interrupted by the bell then, and had to head over to their first lesson – still plotting.

Ms Loftus had said that the cast list of the play would probably go up on the Drama noticeboard some time that day, so Saima and Annabel made a point of detouring past the noticeboard on the way to every lesson that morning. When the bell went for lunch they dashed down to the board again, ignoring the others laughing at them.

By the time Katie, Becky, Megan and Fran caught up there was a huge crowd around the board, a squirming mass desperately trying to read the list. Laughing, Annabel and Saima fought their way back again.

"So? Tell us!" asked Katie excitedly. It had to be good news – Annabel looked positively smug.

"I'm Cinderella! Isn't it brilliant? Oh, it's going to be so coo-ool!" Annabel couldn't resist doing a little twirl in the middle of the corridor. "Go on, Saima, tell them who you are." She nudged Saima, who was looking equally pleased with herself.

"I got the Fairy Godmother. There's a solo song, too."

"And you know what makes it even better?" Annabel beamed. "The prince is Josh

Matthews from Year Eight. He's going to fall in love with me!" Annabel twirled again, so over-excited that she bumped into someone, and Katie had to reach out and steady her so she didn't fall.

Amy Mannering reeled back dramatically, as though Annabel had mortally wounded her, and snarled, "Watch it, moron!" Then she stomped crossly past, with Cara and Emily trailing behind her, twittering.

Annabel and Saima giggled. "Look who didn't get the part she wanted," murmured Annabel to the others, her eyes sparkling. "She's furious!"

"So what part did she get?" Becky asked curiously.

"The Queen – it's not a bad part, but it's not huge, and she wanted *my* part." Annabel hugged herself gleefully as she said this. Her part – she'd done it, she was starring as Cinderella!

*

Amy hadn't had much idea what to do to get the triplets into trouble over their switch, but now that (as she saw it) Annabel had stolen her part, her brain was in overdrive trying to come up with something. She marched out into the playground to find Max, who was mooching along the fence kicking a cola can.

He looked faintly worried as he saw Amy approaching – she practically had steam coming out of her ears, and her pretty face was screwed up and cross.

"We have to tell Mr Hatton what they did!" she spat, as soon as she was within earshot.

Cara and Emily looked at each other anxiously, but left it to Max to point out the problem with this.

He didn't mince words. "Are you mad? You know what he's like. He'll probably put us in detention for telling tales, and then make mean jokes about it in French for the rest of the year, so that everyone knows. No way."

Amy scowled even more, but didn't attempt to argue – Max was right. Mr Hatton was deeply unpredictable, which was why everyone was scared of him.

"Of course," Max mused, "you could just make sure he finds out. Without actually *telling* him."

"How?" Amy asked eagerly, her eyes lighting up.

"Could we get someone else to tell him?" asked Emily hopefully.

"No. You need to tell him without him realizing what you're doing somehow. I know! French tomorrow morning – when he does conversation—"

All three girls groaned. Conversation was Mr Hatton's pet form of torture. At the end of most lessons he would make everyone put their books away, and then he'd pick on people to talk in French. Everyone hated it.

"No, listen. You volunteer, and you bring the subject round to the play. Keep saying about the auditions being on Tuesday and Annabel being Cinderella – he'll work it out."

Cara looked worried. "Isn't he going to smell a rat? No one *ever* volunteers for conversation."

Max smirked at them. "Nope. Sorry to tell you, but everyone in the class knows that Amy shows off all the time." He watched her carefully as he said this, but Amy just stiffened slightly, and said nothing. "If she volunteers to start talking about the play it's because she's in it and she wants everyone to know. Perfectly normal."

Amy clearly didn't want to agree, but couldn't resist the plan. "I don't even know the French for audition," she said grudgingly.

"*L'audition*, I should think," said Max airily. "But you should probably go and look up what you're going to say in the library, if you're going to try it." Then he walked off, smirking to himself. If there was anything better than getting the triplets into trouble, it was getting them into trouble but making someone else do the work for him. . .

Amy hared off, looking determined, but she and Max hadn't realized they were being watched. As the triplets and their friends had come out into the playground, Saima had spotted the little huddle over by the fence. It was very odd for Amy and her bratty mates to be honouring anyone else with their company, and it was positively suspicious for them to be talking to Max − he'd ganged up with them before to get at the triplets. As Amy and Max plotted, Saima caught Annabel's eye and jerked her head in their direction. "Look."

Annabel was too hyper to take it seriously. "They're welcome to him," she giggled.

"I want to know what they're up to," said Saima, as she watched Amy dashing away to the library. "Come on, Bel. We'll be back in a minute," she called to the others, grabbing

Annabel by the arm and making for the main building.

Annabel was still giggling as she and Saima sneaked into the library.

"Ssshhh! Stop it, Bel, they'll hear us!" Saima scooted into position behind a shelf of Biology books and peered round carefully. Annabel crept after her with exaggerated tiptoeing movements, still smirking. They could hear Amy talking from behind the next set of shelves, where the Modern Languages books were.

"It'll be easy. We've got our words written down, so all we have to do is read it out. But make sure you two sound like you're making it up on the spot. Once we've told him that there was an audition for the play on Tuesday after school, and that we're all going to be in it, he's bound to ask if anyone else is. Annabel will have to say yes, and there we go."

Amy chuckled nastily, and Cara and Emily

tittered. Annabel turned back from the gap in the shelves that she'd been peering through, and gazed in horror at Saima. This was a disaster – obviously Max and Amy between them had worked out that the triplets had switched for detention, and now they were aiming to get them into big trouble. Saima and Annabel flattened themselves against the shelves as Amy and the other two went past, then dashed out after them – they had to find a way to stop this happening!

Katie, Becky and the others were chatting happily when Annabel and Saima got back, but one look at the two girls' faces was enough to shut them up.

"What's the matter?" Becky asked anxiously. "You look as though something terrible's happened." She immediately thought of the play. "Did Ms Loftus change her mind?"

"We're dead," Annabel declared – less

dramatically than she usually would; this was too serious for messing about.

Katie clocked her sister's desperate expression. "What? What's happened?"

"Max and Amy know about yesterday, that it wasn't me in detention, and they're going to tell Mr Hatton. They've got this plan and they're going to tell him in French tomorrow and he'll kill us and they'll probably stop me being in the play—" Annabel had to pause here, the words had been spilling out too fast for her to breathe. Her intake of breath was almost a sob, and Becky put an arm round her comfortingly.

Annabel stayed miserably quiet, her head hanging, and everyone looked at Saima for more information. She quickly explained what they'd overheard in the library. "I don't know how we can stop them," she finished despairingly.

Annabel lifted her head. "We can't." She sounded as though she thought the world was about to end.

Katie looked grim. "I'm not going to give Amy Mannering the satisfaction of getting us into trouble. We've got to go and tell Mr Hatton ourselves – before those two do. If Max and Amy go through with that plan it'll be really embarrassing. I don't want to have a massive row with Mr Hatton in front of our whole class."

Everyone shuddered.

"So you really think we have to go and tell him? I'm really sorry, Katie, I didn't mean to get you in trouble too." Annabel's voice was full of horror.

"It was my idea, Bel, don't be a muppet. We'll tell him after school. He might be in a good mood, being about to go home. Let's hope so, anyway." Katie shrugged. "It seemed like such a good plan at the time. Oh, Bel, don't cry!" She'd noticed Annabel's suspiciously bright eyes and pink nose. "Look, we'll grovel, it'll be OK." Katie caught Becky's eye over Annabel's shoulder – she looked doubtful. Katie gave the tiniest eyebrow-shrug, a "well, what else can I say?" face. It had to be OK, somehow. Katie just wasn't quite sure how they were going to pull this one off.

The afternoon seemed to go horribly quickly, and all too soon the triplets were standing outside the staffroom door, gulping in unison. Becky had uncharacteristically told Katie not to be so stupid when she pointed out that, actually, Becky hadn't done anything wrong and didn't need to be there. Somehow it didn't feel right to knock on the staffroom door, so they hung around looking embarrassed until a member of staff galloped up the stairs and gave them a funny look.

Katie swallowed. "Um, I'm sorry to be a nuisance, but would you be able to see if Mr Hatton's there, please?" She was already in buttering-up mode.

After what seemed like ages, the teacher

came back out looking a bit harassed, and said that Mr Hatton was helping Ms Loftus in the hall, so Katie grimly led the way down there instead. They crept round the door, and spotted Ms Loftus and Mr Hatton standing on the stage, apparently transfixed by the ceiling. It turned out they were looking at the stage lights, and Mr Hatton, of all people, was talking in a very professional-sounding way about tightening the spots and adding different coloured gels. Was he helping with the play?

Annabel took a deep breath. "Um, excuse me?"

The teachers turned round, looking surprised.

"Annabel!" Ms Loftus sounded pleased. "We didn't notice you were there. Have you seen the cast list? Congratulations!" She turned to Mr Hatton. "This is Annabel Ryan, she's playing Cinderella. She really shone in the auditions on Tuesday."

Normally Annabel would have been preening at this, but instead she flinched at the dreaded word, Tuesday – would Mr Hatton notice?

It seemed he did. He frowned slightly, and then in a politely interested voice, one that the triplets recognized from French – it meant he was about to go ballistic if he got the wrong answer – he murmured, "Tuesday? Now, that *is* interesting. I had the distinct impression that you were in detention on Tuesday, Annabel."

Annabel, for once, was tongue-tied, but she finally managed to mutter, "Um, yes. I was. But I wasn't. If you see what I mean."

"No." Mr Hatton was now tapping his finger on his chin – another bad sign.

Katie broke in – Annabel obviously wasn't getting anywhere. "We swapped," she admitted, deciding just to get it over with. "I did Annabel's detention so she could go to the audition."

Ms Loftus seemed shocked, and Annabel gave her a miserable, apologetic look.

"Why are you telling me this now?" asked Mr Hatton, sweetly.

Katie flushed, but answered, "Because someone else is going to tell you anyway."

"Well, at least you're honest – sometimes. You didn't consider coming and explaining all this before Tuesday afternoon?"

"We didn't think you'd listen," Annabel whispered unhappily.

This was quite true, of course, and Mr Hatton could see that she meant it. "After your disgraceful behaviour in my lesson, it would have been perfectly reasonable to stop you going to the audition. However, if you'd had the sense to ask, I would have rearranged your detention. But you preferred to be sly and underhand instead." He watched the triplets shrink slightly. "You should be ashamed of yourselves – using your appearance to deceive people like that."

He went on like this for some time, and even Katie was having trouble holding back tears. It made it worse that Ms Loftus was nodding along grimly. Mr Hatton seemed to know an enormous number of words for dishonest, and he used all of them. He finished off by setting each of them a huge chunk of French exercises to do (he apparently knew their textbook off by heart, scarily enough), different bits for each of them, as "Obviously I can't trust you not to copy from each other if I give you the same work to do." He gave Becky slightly less than the others, but told her she should have had the sense to stop them, so he wasn't letting her off.

Eventually, the triplets slunk away, still cringing. It wasn't until they were halfway home that Annabel stopped in the middle of the pavement.

"What?" asked Katie, grumpily. She'd decided that she was definitely never, ever doing anything like that again.

"I've just realized – it worked. He made me feel so awful that I hadn't thought about it, but Amy and Max are going to go through with that stupid plan tomorrow, and it'll all be for nothing. I'm still going to be in the play!"

Chapter Four

Annabel didn't think she'd ever seen anyone look quite so frustrated as Amy at half-past ten on Thursday morning. She and Cara and Emily had been carefully parroting their prepared sentences for ages now, and Mr Hatton was showing no sign of getting the hint. He seemed fairly pleased with their sudden interest in French conversation, but that was about it. Amy lapsed into a mulish silence, and Mr Hatton turned to the rest of the class. He asked, in French, whether anyone else was going to be in the play. The entire class stared back at him with looks of polite incomprehension on their faces. No one had a clue what he'd just said. Mr Hatton sighed, and started to go through his sentence again on the board. As he explained each word, Amy brightened up – Mr Hatton was actually going along the right lines now.

"So—" he turned back from the board – "*Qui d'autre jouera dans la pièce?*"

Several hands went up, Annabel's included, and Amy held her breath. Surely, after all the times she'd said the auditions were on Tuesday after school, he *had* to make the connection? Yes! He was picking on Annabel.

Two minutes later, Amy was practically banging her head against the desk, and Cara and Emily were looking confused. How could a *teacher* be this stupid? All right, he had just told Annabel that her grammar, vocabulary and accent were despicable, which would usually have been quite satisfying, but that wasn't the point right now. And the triplets were looking unbearably smug for some reason. It was almost as though they knew . . .

but they couldn't. Could they? She caught Annabel's eye, and all at once it was obvious that they did. Annabel's triumphant grin just couldn't mean anything else. Amy ground her teeth. How did the triplets *always* manage to come out on top? Well, somehow she was going to get Annabel Ryan – she didn't know how just yet, but darling Cinderella had better watch out. . .

That afternoon was the first rehearsal for the play. Annabel and Saima were in the hall less than two minutes after the bell went. The rest of the cast trickled in gradually, chatting to each other about the play and their parts. Eventually Ms Loftus strode in, looking pleased to see everyone there already. She was followed by various other members of staff – Mr Becket, the Music teacher who'd been at the auditions; Mrs Cranmer, one of the Art teachers; Miss Davies, the Textiles teacher, and, scarily enough, Mr Hatton.

"What's *he* doing here?" muttered Annabel to Saima in horror.

"No idea," Saima mouthed back at once, wide-eyed.

Ms Loftus stood in the middle of the hall, with the other teachers gathered slightly sheepishly around her. "Hello everybody, and welcome to our first rehearsal! Now, we don't have a huge amount of time – only five weeks until the performance!" Everyone groaned. "So we need to work really hard. Because there's a lot to do in a short time, I've been lucky enough to get lots of other staff to help, as you can see. Mrs Cranmer will be doing scenery and Miss Davies will be organizing the costumes, which is great, and they'll be asking for volunteers to help out. They'll be making lists of people at the end of the rehearsal, so have a think about that, please. Mr Becket is in charge of the singing, as you know, and I'm delighted to say that Mr Hatton will be giving me a hand with the direction and the backstage crew."

Mr Hatton smiled grimly, and everyone in the cast stared back, slightly gobsmacked. He was the last teacher they'd expect to be helping with the school play – it was more his style to be complaining about the amount of homework time it took up.

"So, let's get going everyone. Mr Becket has your scripts" – the Music teacher was struggling under a huge pile of paper – "so if you could take one each. And please remember that that is *your only copy*." As a Drama teacher, Ms Loftus was perfectly able to breathe accents of death into those words. "If you lose your script, I will *not* be giving you another one. You'll just have to borrow one and photocopy it."

The entire cast descended on Mr Becket, who had the sense to dump the scripts on the stage and run before he disappeared under the flailing mass. Eventually, everyone had managed to secure a script, and people trotted back to their perches, eager to see how many lines they'd ended up with.

Annabel flicked excitedly through the script, nodding with pleasure as she saw how many of the pages Cinderella appeared on. By about two-thirds of the way through, she was starting to look a little anxious. She looked over at Saima, who was reading her big scene, where she transformed Annabel, and obviously imagining herself in a glittery Fairy Godmother costume.

Saima glanced up, and grinned at her. "Isn't this brilliant? I'm so excited." Then she appeared to read Annabel's mind. "You know, you've got loads of words. It's a fantastic part. And two solos as well."

"Mmmmm." Annabel smiled, but rather worriedly.

Saima looked more carefully at her. "Are you panicking about learning the lines?"

"A bit. I hadn't thought there'd be so many. I'm on almost every page!"

"It'll be OK. You've got Becky and Katie to help you learn them, for a start – my mum and dad are always so busy, I can't see them having much time to test me."

Annabel brightened up. Saima was right. "I bet Katie and Becky will help you too. And I will — we've got one scene we can practise together, anyway." She grinned happily at Saima — this was going to be so cool! Then her smile deepened — Josh Matthews was heading in her direction — was he coming to talk to them?

"Hi! You had a look through the script?"

"Mmm. It's good, isn't it?" Annabel stammered slightly from nervousness — he was so good-looking!

"Did you notice page thirty-six?"

"Er, no, I don't think so." Annabel riffled through the script. The ballroom scene — she smiled to herself, imagining the gorgeous dress she'd be wearing. Oh! She'd just noticed the stage directions — the prince was supposed to kiss Cinderella! Annabel blushed very pink and looked up at Josh. "Oh yes..." she murmured rather lamely. Well, what was she supposed to say when she found out that a boy she really, really liked was going to be kissing her in front of half the school?

Josh grinned, and turned to go. "Well, see you!"

"Um, yeah," Annabel muttered, and gazed after him with a slightly glazed look in her eyes.

"An-na-bel! Wake up!" Saima was giggling. "Stop it, you look as though you're about to fall at his feet. You have to be a *little bit* hard to get!"

Annabel jumped. "Sorry! I just hadn't realized – I suppose it's obvious that the prince kisses Cinderella, but I didn't think about it. Wow." She hugged the script to herself tightly – this play was just getting better and better!

Ms Loftus had given them a quick rundown of this version of *Cinderella* at the audition, so she was eager to get straight on with the play now.

It started with an introductory scene set several years before the rest of the play, when Cinderella was a baby. Annabel kept half an eye on what was happening onstage while she read carefully through her first scene — she didn't want to be like the people up there now. The two Year Nines had had no chance to see what they were saying before they had to say it, and they were stumbling and giggling in embarrassment. The next scene was at the palace, with Amy as the queen. She was good — Annabel had to admit it, grudgingly. She told herself that Amy's stuck-up manners suited the part.

"Very nice, Amy!" Ms Loftus sounded really pleased at the end of the scene, and Amy smiled at her sweetly.

The smile changed to a grimace as she came offstage and headed straight for Annabel. "You see? That's proper acting, Annabel. Ms Loftus is going to be really sorry she picked you for Cinderella. Just try not to ruin the whole thing, OK?" She flounced off before Annabel could think of anything suitably nasty to say back.

"Just ignore her," said Saima. "You'll be brilliant, she'll see," she added loyally. Annabel tried to smile – she *had* been feeling really confident, but Amy had a way of getting to people. It was such a huge part – could she really do it? There was no more time to worry about it, though, her first scene was now. She went up onstage, and tried very hard to concentrate on Saima and Ms Loftus beaming at her, and not see Amy's carefully pitying expression.

Cinderella was meant to be sweeping the kitchen on her own – there wasn't even anyone to keep her company onstage! Annabel gulped, and started off nervously – remember to project her voice, not stare at the ground, put feeling into the words – there was so much to think about! And she had to cope with Ms Loftus calling directions for "blocking", where she wanted Annabel to move. But by the time two Year Nine boys came on as the Ugly Sisters to bully her, Annabel was starting to get into it. Joe and Pete were really fun, and they were overacting massively, so Annabel played up to them – it was so much easier when there was someone else to act with!

"What did you think?" she asked Saima anxiously as soon as she came back into the main hall. "Was I OK? Tell me!"

"Definitely," said Saima firmly. "You were fab. A lot better than Her Majesty over there, so don't let her get to you, all right?"

The rest of the rehearsal went really well, Annabel thought. Ms Loftus did look a bit panicked in some places, but she was still just about smiling by the time she called a halt. Annabel was feeling so upbeat by then that she went a bit overboard when Ms Loftus reminded them about volunteers for backstage crew and set and costumes.

Saima watched in surprise as Annabel

merrily added her entire family to the various lists – Katie to work backstage, Becky to paint the set, her mum to make costumes. Miss Davies looked over Annabel's shoulder as she scrawled Mrs Ryan's name on her list.

"Oh good. Is your mum good at sewing, Annabel? I was hoping someone would volunteer to make your ballgown – I've got an awful lot of costumes to make, and the dress pattern I've got isn't difficult, but it's going to take a bit of time, it's quite fancy."

Quite fancy? Annabel shivered delightedly. She wanted it as fancy as possible. "I'm sure she could make it, Miss Davies. She likes sewing."

Miss Davies lost no time in loading Annabel down with the pattern and the fabric – gorgeous silvery-lilac stuff, with sparkly bits, which had Annabel looking like a Cheshire cat, and Saima just the teensiest bit jealous.

Miss Davies caught the look, though, and grinned at her. "Don't worry, Saima, you've got something along the same lines but in gold – you'll look lovely."

Saima and Annabel walked home in a blissful silence, imagining their beautiful dresses. Shortly before they got to the Ryans' house, Saima woke up enough to say, "I didn't know your mum liked sewing."

"Oh, she does." Annabel nodded happily. This was perfectly true, but when Annabel got home and broke the news of her mother's new role, Mrs Ryan looked horrified.

"Oh, Annabel, why?" she wailed. "I've got loads of work on at the moment, you really should have asked me first."

Annabel looked hurt. "But you like sewing. I thought you'd *want* to make my ballgown."

Mrs Ryan looked at Annabel's hurt face, all huge blue eyes, and backtracked. "Sweetheart, I do want to, it's just that this looks like a really complicated dress to make. I don't want to spoil it for you." She sighed, took a big gulp of coffee, and looked back down at the pattern instructions. "Well, I can try, I suppose. These things always look worse than they really are. But honestly, what on earth's *that* bit?" She stabbed a finger worriedly at a small piece that looked as though it really couldn't fit anywhere on a dress.

Katie and Becky, who'd been watching, peered over at the pattern.

"Twenty-six – waistband reinforcement panel. It's for when Annabel gets fat," giggled Katie.

Annabel looked speculatively at her. "You're helping too, you know."

"What? I'm not making dresses, Bel, you know I'm no good at sewing."

"I put you down for helping backstage. I thought you'd like that. Lights and stuff – you know." Annabel waved a hand airily.

"Oh, great! And what's Becky? Your personal slave?"

Annabel smiled at Becky. "I said you'd

help paint scenery. That's OK, isn't it? You like art, and you like Mrs Cranmer – she's organizing it."

Becky looked pleased – unlike Katie, she wasn't bothered by Annabel arranging stuff for her, as long as it was something she'd like! "Cool. Do you think I could ask David if he wants to help too?"

Annabel rolled her eyes. "Course you can, silly. More the better, I should think. You can go and paint together – awww!"

Becky just grinned good-naturedly. She was getting used to Annabel's teasing, and she knew it was partly because her sister was a weeny bit jealous.

"Really, Annabel," Mrs Ryan was trying hard to sound cross in the face of Annabel's enthusiasm. "You should have asked everybody before you did all this. I know you're excited about the play, but you can't just assume that everybody else will be too."

Annabel looked innocent. "But you are,

aren't you?" she asked, gazing hopefully round at her mother and sisters. "And you will do it?"

"Yes," chorused her family, in long-suffering tones.

Annabel beamed. Perhaps this was not the moment to admit that she'd volunteered Fran and Megan as well. . .

Chapter Five

"Great news," said Mrs Ryan at breakfast the next morning. "I spoke to your Auntie Janet last night after you'd gone to bed and told her all about the ballgown and the play. She's agreed to help me put it together, Bel, and suggested we bring the pattern and everything with us when we all go up to London."

Annabel promptly spilt milk down her sweatshirt. "Auntie Jan's going to help? Oh, Mum, that's fantastic."

"Hey, watch it!" The milk was still dripping, and Katie was trying to keep her sleeves out of the way. "Bel! Wake up and look what you're doing, will you?"

Becky dived for a cloth to wipe up Annabel, and Mrs Ryan just stared resignedly at the state of the breakfast table. Annabel ignored the carnage around her entirely, and concentrated on the important issues. "Auntie Jan's so good with clothes and stuff – my dress'll be perfect!"

Her mother made a face. "Well, thank you too, Annabel. I'm not that bad!"

Annabel wasn't listening. She'd been excited enough about the trip before, but the thought of having super-fashionable Auntie Jan make her dress had pushed her into bliss. "I can't believe we're going to London *tomorrow*! Actually" – she was suddenly serious – "I need to plan what clothes to take." And she was dead silent from then on, gazing into space as she worked out her wardrobe. She only woke up halfway to school, when she'd covered every possible combination, and then she started dancing along the pavement.

Katie looked at her irritably. "Bel, will you please try to get your head in gear for school? Remember what happened on Monday? I know it's turned out OK in the end, but I'm not going through that again. Just calm down."

Annabel gave her sister a shocked look. This was truly grumpy behaviour from Katie, and it was difficult for Annabel to process someone being grumpy when she felt so bouncy herself.

"What's the matter?" she asked curiously, walking backwards to stare into her sister's face. "Why are you all cross? Aren't you excited about tomorrow?"

"I'm not cross," Katie muttered crossly.

"You are."

"I'm not."

"Yes, you are."

"If I *say* I'm not cross, I'm not cross, OK?" Katie snapped.

"*Fine*, then. I was only trying to be nice." Annabel stomped off ahead.

Becky decided it was definitely time to intervene. "Don't you want to go to London, Katie? It's going to be fun."

"Huh."

"It will! What's the matter?"

Katie huffed crossly. "It was bad enough when it was a whole weekend of shopping, but now we've got to sit around while Mum and Auntie Jan make *dresses* for Annabel. I'd rather stay at home."

Becky gave her a troubled look. "It won't be like that! It's nearly Christmas, we're going to do loads of present-shopping. Don't you want to get something nice for Megan?" she wheedled.

"Course I do!" Katie snapped back. "But it's all going to be clothes shops and stupid girly stuff – really boring."

"Speak for yourself," muttered Annabel, who'd let them catch up again. She was feeling grumpy herself after her spat with Katie, but she couldn't stay down for long with the prospect of a day's shopping. Everywhere would be all Christmassy, with loads of party outfits in the shops, and decorations all over the place. If there was anything better than just plain shopping, it was shopping at Christmas. She looked sympathetically at Katie. How awful to be depressed by shopping! Suddenly she remembered that Katie had sorted out her audition-disaster for her, and felt guilty. She gave her sister a hug. "It won't all be clothes, honestly. We'll go to places you like too. And I'll be good today, I promise. Perfect little angel until home time, and then I'll go crazy. OK?"

Annabel managed to keep her word – just. When she felt the excitement bubbling up (a particular problem in geography – it was a mystery at Manor Hill how Mrs Travers managed to be quite so amazingly boring) she looked very firmly at Katie, and thought about her being sweet enough to do a detention for her. As soon as she got outside the school gates, though, she gave in completely. She shoved her bag into Becky's arms, dashed down the road far enough to find a clear spot, and actually turned a cartwheel to work off some of the accumulated craziness. She was giggly and silly all the rest of the way, and when they got home she dashed upstairs immediately.

The triplets' mum, who'd seen her go past only as a streak of blonde hair, looked worried. "What's the matter with Annabel?"

"Nothing," explained Becky, grinning. "She's just desperate to get changed out of school clothes and get the weekend started."

She was interrupted by Annabel, hanging over the banisters. "Come on! You have to change too, I don't even want to *see* school uniform. I wish we lived in America."

She disappeared again, leaving her mother looking confused. "What's America got to do with anything?"

Katie smiled understandingly. "They don't

wear school uniform over there. We'll be down soon."

Annabel's giggliness could be very infectious – if you weren't in a bad mood to start with – and she'd tried so hard to be sensible all day that Katie had forgiven her entirely and started to get excited about the weekend too. After all, it would be fun to see Auntie Jan, and Becky was right, she *did* need to get Christmas presents. The three girls spent teatime giggling so much that Becky got hiccups from trying to laugh through her shepherd's pie. It took them longer than usual to eat, but as soon as they had choked down enough, Annabel dragged the other two upstairs. "Come on! I've got really important stuff to talk about!"

Becky sat down on her bed, clutching Orlando, and cooing sweet nothings in his ear. "What is it, Bel?"

"Christmas-present shopping!" Annabel announced importantly.

"We know!" Katie looked unimpressed.

"What I mean is, we ought to make a plan. There's no point going shopping with no idea what you want to buy. I mean, a bit of impulse buying is good, definitely, but we ought to know what we think people want for Christmas, or we'll end up with three things for Saima, say, and nothing for Megan."

Katie nodded – for once Annabel was right. How did she manage to be sensible and organized only when it came to shopping?

Annabel rounded on Becky. "And you've got a massive problem," she declared, waving a finger in her sister's face in a doom-laden way.

Becky shrank back – not actually because she was worried by Bel, she was too used to her being overdramatic for that, but because she could tell that Orlando was objecting to fingers being waved in front of his jaws, and was preparing to have a piece out of her sister. "What?" she enquired curiously.

"What are you going to buy David for

Christmas?" Annabel folded her arms and looked down at Becky smugly.

"Oh. I hadn't thought. I don't know, really." A worried expression appeared on Becky's face. What on earth *was* she going to get him?

"You see? We need to make a list of everyone we want to get presents for, and start thinking before tomorrow." Annabel smiled sweetly. "You two need to start thinking what to give *me*, as well. I could show you some stuff in magazines if you like." She started over to the teetering pile of magazines by her bed, but Katie grabbed her and bundled her over to the big table.

"*No,* thank you. We want you concentrating for now. You can drop hints later, when we've got everyone else sorted." Katie was in organizing mode now, and she grabbed paper and pens for list-making. "Let's start off with making a list of everybody we need to get presents for."

"Well, each other, obviously," Becky

suggested. "But you want to leave that till last, don't you."

Katie grinned. "Oh, I don't mind discussing *you*, I just want Bel's mind clear, that's all. Got any ideas what you want?"

Annabel gasped indignantly, and would have protested, but Katie put her hand over her mouth. "Shut up, Bel, or I'll tickle you." She waved her fingers threateningly close to Annabel's neck. Annabel was so ticklish that if she was in the right mood even this could send her into hysterics. She struggled feebly, and made pleading eyes at Katie.

Katie released her. Annabel sighed resignedly and she started making the list. "OK. Saima. Megan and Fran, yes? *David*—" with a teasing look at Becky.

Becky refused to rise. "Mum, Dad, Auntie Jan, Grandma and Grandpa, Nan."

Katie came round to look over Annabel's shoulder. "What on earth are we going to get Mum?"

"Haven't a clue. But we should probably get Auntie Janet something wedding-y, do you think?" Becky suggested. "You can get lots of books on how to organize weddings, I've seen them." Auntie Janet was getting married to her fiancé, Mark, in the spring, and she was full of wedding plans already.

Katie pointed at their grandparents' names. "Mum'll probably have good ideas about what to get. But her present's really difficult."

"Mmm. It would be nice to get her a surprise that she actually did really like." Becky frowned. "She's not easy to get presents for."

Annabel nibbled her pen. A tiny scrap of an idea was gathering. She nibbled harder. They were going shopping with Auntie Jan. . . Auntie Jan who was very, *very* similar-looking to Mum – different hair, but their figures and faces were almost as identical as the triplets' were. Mum was always complaining that she had nothing nice to wear, but she didn't really enjoy clothes shopping all that much (which Annabel found very hard to understand). Mum said she always ended up trying on things that looked lovely on the hanger but horrible on her. So. . . The idea was slipping round the edges of her brain. . .

"I've got it! We get rid of Mum somehow" – Annabel was still sketchy on the details – "and then we borrow Auntie Jan!"

Katie and Becky looked at her sceptically.

"What?" said Katie witheringly.

Annabel sighed. They were so *slow* sometimes. "We go to a clothes shop," she said, her tone indicating that they were idiots and she was talking in words of one syllable on purpose, "and we get Auntie Jan to try on clothes so we can see what would look good on Mum!" She sat back looking pleased with herself.

"Bel, that's a brilliant idea," breathed Becky delightedly. "We should be able to get her something perfect."

Katie grinned. "I've changed my mind — pass those magazines, Becky. OK, Bel, here's your reward. What do you want for Christmas?"

Chapter Six

"Ummm." Annabel fiddled with her hairclips. "'It's not fair, the invitation was addressed to me as well'?"

"Nope, that's in about three lines' time. It's 'I really wish I could go to the ball'." Katie looked round the script at Annabel. "You're getting better though. You know what the lines are – now it's just a case of getting them in the right order. . ."

Becky giggled – Annabel's affronted face was very funny.

The triplets and their mum were on the train to London, sitting round a table sharing some cookies that Mrs Ryan had bought at the station as a treat. Katie was testing Annabel on her words for the play, and it wasn't going too well.

"You know," said Katie thoughtfully. "I think the problem is that you're only learning your own words."

Annabel glared at her, even her hair looking irritable. She hated being wrong. "What, I'm supposed to learn everybody else's words as well? Come on, Katie!"

"No, no, no. I mean, you know your lines, and you know *approximately* when you're supposed to say them" – Annabel snarled – "but it would be better if you said the lines as though you were actually answering the person before you. So you *do* need to know their line too. Or at least know what it is they're trying to say."

Annabel was silent. She very much wanted to tell Katie not to be so stupid, but it sounded horribly as though she might be right. Mum was nodding as though she thought so too. She stuck out her hand. "Give it here."

Katie handed the script over, and Annabel

looked down at it gloomily. Still, the more she did now, the less she'd have to worry about it later on that day while they were shopping. She didn't want any distractions. She scowled down at the script and concentrated hard until Mum tapped her on the shoulder – they were pulling into Paddington station. She stuffed the script away in her bag quickly, and jumped up to help the others get the bags down from the rack over their heads.

"Bel, how come you need so much stuff when we're only going for one night?" asked Becky, nearly collapsing under the weight of Annabel's rucksack.

Annabel looked at her, honestly confused. "Well, how do I know what I'm going to feel like tomorrow? If I only brought one outfit, it might be totally wrong for the way I'm feeling, and then I'd just be really weird all day."

Katie and Becky exchanged looks, and Katie coughed suspiciously, but they wisely decided not to say anything.

The triplets looked around excitedly as they walked through the station. They'd been to London before, to see Auntie Janet, and Dad had taken them all to see a show a couple of years earlier, but it was still an event. They attracted quite a lot of attention themselves – several people did a double take as they saw the three girls go by.

Mum drilled the triplets firmly on where they were going as they waited for a tube to arrive. She knew that Annabel especially had an amazing knack of getting lost – just because she got distracted so easily. At least if she knew where the flat was she had a chance of getting back there – and Mrs Ryan had made sure Auntie Janet's number was in Annabel's mobile. Eventually the train roared into the station, pouring out shoppers and tourists. They had to wait for a whole party of French schoolkids to go past them, giggling and pointing, before they could get on.

"Come on, Bel!" snapped Katie, feeling

ruffled. Annabel was still making faces back at the last of the French boys.

The train was quite full so they clutched desperately at one of the rails, holding on to each other and swaying round the bends, giggling. Luckily it wasn't a long way to the stop nearest to Auntie Janet's flat.

As they walked up the street towards her building they could see a figure waving madly at the window. Then it disappeared, and the front door opened as they got to it, with Auntie Jan, breathless, hanging on to the handle.

"You got here! Oh, this is so nice, it's ages since I've seen you. Come on!" And she dashed back up the stairs, grabbing a couple of bags and calling, "Mark! They're here!"

The triplets had only met Mark once before. He'd seemed OK, but they hadn't really talked to him, so they hung back a little. Mum and Auntie Jan were hugging and talking excitedly, and the triplets weren't quite sure what to do.

Mark grinned briefly at them, and then groaned – he was playing a PlayStation game, and he'd obviously just mucked up. Katie wandered over to look at the screen – it was a football game that they had at home. Mark was on a pretty high level, she noted – quite impressed.

"Sorry." He finally stood up. "Er – you got here OK, then?" he stared at them for a moment, looking nonplussed. "Look, I know this must be really irritating, but I can't work out which is which. You're Katie, right?" He *was* actually pointing to Katie, but she glared at him anyway. She really hated it when people got confused. Becky saw the look in her eyes and decided to head her off in case she said something snappish – that wouldn't be a good way to start off the visit.

"That's right. And I'm Becky and this is Annabel."

Annabel smiled politely. How could anyone not remember who *she* was?

"OK. Right." Mark could obviously sense the atmosphere. "Sorry. Er, would anyone like a drink?" He bolted into the kitchen.

"Be nice!" Becky murmured, frowning at Katie.

Katie sighed. "Oh, all right. You didn't have to cut me off like that, you know, I wasn't going to say anything." Becky gave her a disbelieving look. "Well, nothing rude. Come on, let's go and get a drink." She led the way into the kitchen.

Luckily, Katie spotted a photo on a board in the kitchen – Mark had run the London marathon. She was even more impressed, and by the time Mum and Auntie Janet stopped catching up and came to find them all, she and Mark were deep in a discussion about exercise routines, while Annabel and Becky pored over one of the piles of wedding magazines they'd discovered on an old armchair in the corner.

Auntie Jan peered over their shoulders.

"Oh, no! I'm not getting married in a meringue, Annabel, no way."

"What is your dress going to be like?" Annabel asked eagerly.

"I'm not totally sure yet, but if we go past any wedding shops today, I'll show you the kind of thing I'm looking for. Come on, we've got loads of shopping to do."

Auntie Janet led them on another tube ride to Covent Garden. She knew Annabel and Becky would like all the cool clothes shops there, but she was hoping that Katie might find it fun to look at some of the places that sold gadgets and sports stuff too. Katie looked doubtful as they came out of the tube station – clothes, clothes and more clothes. She sighed. She had a feeling it was going to be a long day. Annabel was in seventh heaven as they headed towards the market, ooohing at all the Christmas lights, and pointing out shoes, and feathery handbags, and a whole lot of what Katie mentally classed as "Annabel–stuff". When she squeaked, "Oh, look!" for what seemed like the millionth time, Katie was unenthusiastic.

"What?"

"A whole shop full of *Tintin* stuff! Do you want to go in? Mum, did you see? It's a really cool shop for Katie!"

Katie perked up. Annabel was right! "Bel, you star, I didn't even see it. Please, please, can we go in?" She'd loved the *Tintin* books for ages, and the shop looked fantastic.

"David likes *Tintin*," said Becky excitedly. "I could get his Christmas present here."

It turned out to be a fab present shop. Katie, Becky and Annabel were darting about all over the place, dragging each other to look at things. Annabel wasn't a huge *Tintin* fan, but she *was* a shopping fan, and she really entered into the spirit of present-buying. The assistant was looking a bit bewildered – it wasn't a very big shop, and the triplets certainly filled it up.

"Katie, look at this!" Annabel pointed to the

Tintin watch that Becky was holding, and stood back with her head on one side. Katie's reaction was crucial.

"Wow!" Katie took it longingly, and Annabel and Becky nodded in approval – one Christmas present solved!

As Katie wandered off to gaze happily at the posters, Annabel turned to Becky.

"So we'll buy that together for Katie?" Becky sounded pleased – sometimes it was hard to choose presents for Katie, because they weren't as into sporty things as she was.

"Definitely. She seemed to really like it. Have you found anything for David?"

"I'm not sure. What about this?" Becky showed Annabel a mug with some of the book, characters on.

Annabel chewed her lower lip thoughtfully. "It's OK, but a mug's a bit, well, *boring*."

"Mmmm – I just don't know what to choose. Katie, tell me what to get for David," Becky called over to her sister as she put the mug back, frowning. She certainly didn't want the first present she got David to be boring.

"You've been to his house, haven't you?" Katie asked thoughtfully. "If we had the space in our room, I'd love one of those posters."

"Oooh yes!" agreed Annabel, nodding like mad. "Then every time he looks at it he'll think of you!"

Becky inspected the poster Katie was pointing out – Tintin and his dog in huge puffy orange spacesuits – and looked slightly insulted. The other two cracked up.

"Sorry – I didn't mean it like that!" Annabel sniggered.

"It really is a cool poster, Becky. I'd get it for him."

They ended up with the poster, Katie's watch, and quite a few bits that Mum wouldn't let them see and that Katie suspected were for her stocking – and maybe Becky's too, as Tintin's dog was very cute.

After the *Tintin* shop Annabel spotted a stall

full of mobile phone accessories – perfect for Saima. Luckily she knew exactly what phone her friend had, so she could get her a new cover – she'd had her silver one for ages.

"The glitter one, or that one with the purple flowers?" Annabel asked everyone, dithering. The problem was, she knew Saima would like them both.

"What colour's her favourite bag?" put in Auntie Jan.

"Oh, she's got a new purple one – brilliant!"

Annabel happily paid for the flowery phone cover. Good! Now that they'd got a few of the other presents sorted, she reckoned they ought to get on to their plan for Mum's present. She beckoned Katie and Becky into a huddle. "We've got to get rid of Mum!"

"Maybe we could suggest she goes and has a coffee or something?" Becky said doubtfully.

"No." Katie shook her head. "Too obvious we've got a plan."

"Hey, catch up you three!" Auntie Janet was

waving. "You're coming with me for a bit – your mum wants to go and look at presents for you."

Annabel beamed at the others. Fantastic! And presents as well! She just hoped that Mum had been listening properly earlier on. She and Katie and Becky tried not to look too excited as Mum disappeared off – they couldn't wait to let Auntie Janet in on the plan.

As soon as Mum had gone, Auntie Janet turned back to them, looking suspicious. "What are you three planning? Annabel, you look too smug for it to be anything sensible."

"No, it's *really* sensible, honestly. We just need to borrow you without Mum knowing, and she's given us the perfect chance. Come on!"

She led the way into a shop she'd spotted earlier on, full of the kind of clothes Mum liked but never really had the confidence to buy for herself.

"Annabel, where are we going? You won't fit

this stuff, and I don't think they have a teen range. . ." protested Auntie Jan.

"It's not for us," Katie put in, propelling their aunt along from the other side. "It's for Mum!"

Katie and Becky gave Auntie Jan a quick rundown of the plan and marshalled her to the fitting rooms, while Annabel nosed along the rails looking for likely stuff.

Five minutes later a walking pile of clothes appeared outside the fitting-room door. "This'll do to start with," said Annabel cheerfully, dumping all the stuff on a bench. "Why haven't you taken your coat off?"

Auntie Janet looked down at the pile in horror. "Annabel! This'll take *years* to try on. And look at it, it's all so – not black!" Auntie Janet almost always wore black, or sometimes grey when she fancied a change. Bright colours weren't her thing at all.

"I know. Mum really likes bright clothes, but she doesn't buy them because she thinks she'll look washed out. She just needs the right ones, that's all. And that's where you come in." Annabel grabbed a couple of tops to start with and pushed Auntie Jan into the changing room.

She came out a few minutes later to face the triplets, who were sitting on the bench looking critical. Annabel stood up, folded her arms and put her head on one side. "Could you at least try to smile?" she asked acidly. "It's hard to tell when you look like it actually hurts."

Auntie Jan muttered something, and fingered the burnt-orange fabric in distaste. "OK. Pretending for the moment that I would actually wear *any* of this, what kind of thing are you aiming to give your mum? Everyday clothes, party stuff, what?"

The triplets looked thoughtful. They hadn't really got that far. Annabel glanced at the others enquiringly as she answered. "Something in between? Not hanging round the house clothes, but she doesn't really go out to parties much. I suppose some of these sparkly things might not be quite right." She stroked a sequinned top regretfully, and picked up a flowery dress instead. "This one?" she asked Katie and Becky.

"Yeah, I've always thought Mum wants to look like a walking rosebush, Bel. No," said Katie firmly.

"I think Katie's right," Becky put in. "Mum wouldn't wear that very often."

Annabel frowned to herself, and looked carefully at the pile of clothes. Maybe she had gone a bit mad with some of them. "How about this?" She picked up a pretty blue cardigan with a velvet ribbon round the edges. "She could wear that with jeans, or a skirt. It's, um, *versatile*."

Katie and Becky nodded approvingly. They could imagine Mum in that.

Annabel still made Auntie Jan try five more outfits before they were happy, though. As she said, they didn't want to miss anything. By the time they met up with Mum again, Auntie Jan was looking limp and demanding coffee.

Mum gave them a suspicious look. "What have you been doing? Did Annabel try and buy something really silly?"

Annabel just clutched the bag with the blue cardigan and a striped silk scarf in, and grinned knowingly at the others. Sometimes, even *she* found it hard to believe just how clever she was.

Chapter Seven

The triplets didn't get much sleep that night. They were sharing the sofabed in the front room and the duvet just wasn't quite big enough for three. Becky was in the middle, so she was toasty, but every time Annabel and Katie yanked the duvet over to their own sides she got elbowed! They'd finished off the evening by watching a film from the sofabed on Mark's DVD player – he had a really good film collection. In fact, there were so many things they fancied watching that they ended up tossing a coin and Katie's choice won – *Jaws*. Although it was a really old film the triplets had never seen it. Becky had thought that it wouldn't really be all that scary – it was ancient, and the special effects would be really bad, she reckoned. Actually, she didn't see very many of them. She watched the first quarter of an hour, and then she had to dive under the duvet and have a running commentary from Katie and Annabel instead.

They were still asleep the next morning when an enticing smell wafted into the living room, and they were sitting at the kitchen table within minutes. Mum wasn't up yet, so the triplets told Mark about their shopping success the day before while they wolfed down a fry-up.

"So, did you get everything you wanted?"

Annabel quickly swallowed down a bite of bacon sandwich. "Yup, presents for everybody. People at school, and we got something for you and Auntie Jan. Oh, and we got the best present for Mum, she's going to love it." She nipped back into the living room and found the bag, carefully unfolding the layers of tissue paper round the blue cardigan.

"Nice," said Mark, stroking it. "Very soft."

Annabel looked at him, expecting more. "Is that all you can say?" she asked disgustedly, while Becky and Katie giggled – her face was so funny. Mark looked apologetic and shrugged. Annabel sighed in an "I give up!" sort of way and refolded the cardigan lovingly. "I can't believe it. A whole day of shopping, and I didn't buy anything for me!"

Katie and Becky exchanged smug looks. Annabel didn't know that while she'd been choosing clothes for Auntie Jan to try on, they'd spotted a jewellery display, with a necklace on it just like one she'd pointed out in one of her magazines. There'd been a bracelet too, but they didn't have enough money to get it – so Auntie Jan had volunteered to get it as her Christmas present for Annabel.

When Mum and Auntie Jan finally surfaced, also drawn by the breakfast smell, they were keen to get down to work on the dress, and they commandeered the kitchen table and most of the living-room floor. Annabel was eager to help, as she really wanted to see her dress taking shape, but Becky and Katie began to feel they were rather in the way after they'd been shrieked at for nearly treading on the fabric several times. Becky fetched a book from her bag, and curled minutely into the corner of the sofa, reckoning that if she didn't extend any part of her body beyond the furniture she had to be safe. Katie wasn't feeling like sitting still, though. After shopping all day yesterday she felt like doing something active. She could never live in a flat, she decided. Window boxes were useless for playing football in.

Mark laughed at her the next time she passed his armchair. "You look like a caged tiger. Want to go out? I'm supposed to be playing football with some mates in the park in half an hour – we could go and have a kick about first, if you've got stuff it's OK to play in."

Katie was into her bag and into the bathroom

and out again changed in about thirty seconds. Mark looked a bit gobsmacked.

"I'll take that as a yes then. Come on."

When they returned a couple of hours later the others were looking triumphant. All the pattern pieces had been cut out on the fabric and marked up, and they'd started tacking the different parts of the dress together. Annabel was standing on the coffee table wearing it while Mum and Auntie Janet crawled round her with mouthfuls of pins.

"Is it meant to look like that?" Katie asked doubtfully.

The dress wasn't immediately saying magical ballgown to *her* – there were too many ends sticking out.

Annabel rolled her eyes. "It's inside out, dimwit."

"Oh, OK. Well it's very nice then."

The exercise (and the admiring comments from Mark's mates about her ball skills) had left Katie feeling much more relaxed. She joined Becky on the sofa with a football magazine and a sandwich, and listened to Becky testing Annabel on her lines.

"'Oh, Your Highness' – that's when we kiss, Auntie Jan! Josh is so good-looking, you wouldn't believe. Will you come and see the play? Pleeeease?"

"Mmmmpf." Auntie Jan couldn't speak for pins, but she was nodding.

"Cool. It's going to be really good, the whole thing. Katie and Becky are helping too, you know."

"Like we had a choice," Katie muttered.

By the time they had to head back to the station to go home the dress was nearly finished – it was just the final details like the hemming and adding some ribbon rosebuds that Annabel had bought the day before, dithering over shades of purple ribbon until Katie and Becky had seriously considered trying to set off the fire alarm in the fabric shop.

"See you in a few weeks!" Annabel said happily as the triplets hugged Auntie Jan goodbye on the doorstep.

"Definitely – after all my hard work I have to see you in that dress. Bye! See you soon!"

On Monday after school Annabel dragged Katie and Becky along to the meeting to find out what they could do to help with the play. Luckily for Annabel, Fran and Megan were keen to help too, so no one noticed that she'd volunteered them anyway. When David found out from Becky that they were all going to be helping, probably in lunch hours, he said he'd like to join in too, so it was a biggish group that trooped into the hall that afternoon.

"Oh look, Annabel's brought her fan club!" Amy said snidely as they passed her.

"Least I've got one!" chirped Annabel cheerfully. She was looking forward to Ms Loftus seeing the workforce she'd found.

The Drama teacher was gratifyingly pleased,

and Annabel preened happily. Becky, David and Fran went off to the art studio with Mrs Cranmer to discuss the sets, and Katie and Megan reported rather nervously to Mr Hatton.

Fortunately, he was in a good mood for once. "Any idea what you'd like to do? Lighting? Sound? Stagehands? We need a prompt, too."

All the others in the group were boys, and they seemed keen on the technical bits like lighting. Katie thought that would be quite fun, but when Mr Hatton mentioned prompting she jumped at the chance – she'd been enjoying testing Annabel on her words, and she liked the idea of being the one to rescue anybody who dried up onstage. After a whispered discussion with Megan, who thought it sounded OK, she volunteered them both.

"Excellent. Assistant Stage Managers, both of you. That means prompting, cuing the stage effects, making sure the actors are in the right place, that kind of thing. We'll get you some runners for the performance as well, so you can send them to chase the actors up."

"Becky and Fran and David might do that," Katie suggested. "They're working on scenery now, but they'll be free for the performance." This was starting to sound really good fun – being an ASM seemed to mean you were allowed to boss people around as much as possible!

They all met up and went back to the triplets' house afterwards – they had asked their mum, so she wasn't too shocked when seven people arrived wanting drinks and biscuits. Becky, David and Fran squashed up on the sofa, with a sketchpad they'd borrowed from Annabel. Mrs Cranmer had told them they could be responsible for the set for the ballroom scene and they were really excited. Fran was brilliant at drawing, and soon she was sketching out ideas.

"A big mantelpiece, like this, look, and some portraits, and big vases of flowers—"

"Oh, I thought that was a feather duster," said David, craning his neck to look from another angle.

Becky dug David in the ribs. "Shut up, silly. You knew perfectly well it was flowers. If you're not careful Fran'll make you model for all the portraits."

"Oooh, Fran, you should make all the portraits of the teachers. That would be so funny!" suggested Annabel excitedly. "See how many of them guess!"

It seemed as though the play was shaping up really well, and Annabel was so glad that all her friends were involved too. The only thing that spoilt all the fun a little was that Dad wouldn't be there to see her. She'd been emailing him all about it, and when she checked her messages that evening there was a new one from him.

Hi Bel!

How's everything going? Have you learnt all your words yet? Mum has promised to send me loads of photos of the play, and you in this fantastic dress – I'm so sorry that I can't be there. We're really busy again, and after I had that extra break at half-term, coming home for Christmas just isn't an option this year. Mum's been giving me loads of ideas for Christmas presents though – I think I've got everything sorted. I don't know what I'd do without internet shopping! Oh, nearly forgot – does your computer have a microphone? Can you record yourself saying some of your lines from the play for me, and singing your songs? That way I'll get a bit of a flavour of it. And make sure you get a copy of the video – I bet the school will do one. That can be my Christmas present from you.

Lots of love, Dad

Annabel made a face at the screen. They did have a microphone attached to the computer, but it wasn't very good – and it wasn't nearly the same as having Dad really there. She sighed. The triplets had had to get used to missing him. It had been really hard for Katie recently with Dad missing all her football matches. He was really into sporty stuff and he used to play football with Katie a lot, but he loved seeing Annabel doing stuff like this too. He was always telling her she'd be a star if she just never gave up.

Then she smiled – Dad's email had reminded her of her dress. It was all finished now, and it was hanging up in the wardrobe in Mum's room. Annabel quickly sent off a reply to Dad, promising to do a recording soon. Then she turned the computer off and raced down the steps from the loft – she just had to go and see it again! It was so perfect. She didn't put it on, just lifted it very carefully out of the wardrobe and laid it on the bed so she could stroke it. The silvery–lilac fabric shimmered as she ran her hand down the folds admiringly. It was so unfair that she wouldn't get to keep it! After the play it would become part of the school costume store – even though she knew that it wouldn't fit her for long it was still going to be a wrench. And the idea of somebody else wearing *her* dress was just horrible!

Chapter Eight

"Bel! Bel, where are you?" Katie was calling up the stairs for her. It was time to leave for school, and Annabel was actually looking forward to it. Not only was there a rehearsal that afternoon, but everyone seemed to be getting into a Christmassy mood now that there were only three weeks left until the end of term – even the teachers! OK, this meant that Mr Hatton was having a blitz on "festive vocabulary" in French (Annabel was sick to death of hanging *tresse* on the *sapin de Noël*), but everyone seemed to have lightened up suddenly. Manor Hill was trying to raise enough money to build a swimming pool, which was what the ticket money from the play would be used for, and there was going to be a Christmas Fair on the Saturday after the play, too. Loads of lessons were being borrowed for Fair stuff, and Annabel was all for it.

That afternoon's rehearsal was meant to be a full run-through — the first one. Now that Annabel had almost entirely learnt her words (she only made the odd mistake, and she could generally catch herself and work out what she'd done wrong before Katie had to prompt her) the rehearsals were getting better and better. Not having to look at the script meant that Annabel could concentrate on moving more naturally, and looking at the faces of the people she was talking to, as she would in real life. This was especially good in her scenes with the prince, aka Josh Matthews. Annabel giggled — she was quite happy to look at his face as much as possible. . .

When she and Saima got to the hall Ms

Loftus was running round like a mother hen, looking panicked, and all the cast were feverishly flicking through their scripts, as this was meant to be a no-books rehearsal, and it seemed to have crept up on everybody. By the time they got to the second half, Ms Loftus was looking a bit calmer, but quite a lot of the cast were developing clever techniques for hiding their scripts up their sleeves and writing their lines on their arms. Annabel was feeling smugly virtuous, and *very* grateful to Katie and Becky for spending all that time helping her learn her words.

Not everyone had been so successful. Annabel tried not to look smug as Amy stumbled through her scene with Josh. She obviously hadn't got a Katie to point out the trick about learning your cues as well as your lines, and she kept mixing up which line went where. Josh was sighing dramatically every time she made a mistake, which was wrong-footing her even more.

Eventually Ms Loftus called a halt. "Amy, this is a *run-through*. You ought to know your lines by now. I need you word-perfect for the next rehearsal, you're letting everyone down. Josh, well done."

Josh managed to look modest, long-suffering and very hard-working all at once – it was quite impressive.

"I know I *ought* to feel sorry for Amy," Saima purred. "But somehow I just *don't*. Strange, isn't it?" She beamed at Emily and Cara, who were quite obviously eavesdropping, and preparing to carry tales back to Amy. They didn't have a words problem, they were only being onlookers with the odd line to say here and there.

Annabel smirked at the pair of them. "Poor Amy. Learning lines is *so* difficult. I'm sure she just needs to put a bit of effort in and she'll be fine."

They watched as Emily and Cara scuttled off to meet Amy when she came offstage.

"We shouldn't stir, should we?" Annabel said in a very serious voice.

"Nope," agreed Saima, grinning.

Josh followed Amy off the stage and passed close by Saima and Annabel.

"Hi Annabel! Did you think that went OK?" He smiled charmingly at her, but practically ignored Saima.

Annabel flushed slightly pink. "Yes, it was great — you know your lines really well."

"I'm really enjoying being in this play, are you?" He lounged up against the wall next to them, as though he was settling in for a good chat. "Have you done lots of acting before?"

"Not really. I've done more dancing than acting. How about you?"

"Yeah, I've done some acting. I go to a stage school on Saturdays. I've done a couple of commercials, you know, that kind of thing. . ." Josh looked away casually, but turned back quick enough to see if she was impressed.

She was, very, but she was trying desperately

119

to stay calm. "That sounds cool. Was it hard work?"

"Josh!" An extremely icy voice spoke from behind them. It was Julianne, Josh's girlfriend, and she didn't look happy. She smiled in a polite but very unfriendly way at Annabel and Saima. "Are you coming? We're all sitting over there." She indicated their group of Year Eight mates.

Annabel noticed that although she *sounded* bolshy, she was twisting her hands nervously behind her back, and her teeth were biting into her lower lip. Julianne was really nervous! She wondered why – it looked like Julianne wasn't sure what Josh's reaction was going to be.

Josh scowled. "OK, OK, I'm coming. Are you my mum or something?" He turned back and aimed a high-power smile at Annabel.

Julianne hovered for a moment longer, but Josh ignored her and she sheepishly slunk away, casting a look back at Josh that reminded Annabel of one of Becky's cute puppy posters.

She didn't know whether to feel sorry for Julianne, or gratified that Josh would rather talk to her than his supposed girlfriend. Being gratified won.

"Sorry – she's so clingy, she goes all weird if I talk to any other girls. It's stupid, I mean, it's not as if she's got anything to be jealous of, is it?" Josh smiled at Annabel as he said this, in a way that suggested Julianne might actually have quite a lot to worry about.

"No," said Annabel, smiling back. "We're just talking, aren't we?" she cooed.

Unfortunately Miss Davies called Josh over to go and try on his costume just at that moment. Annabel watched him go, her mind racing. She wasn't really sure what all that meant. She turned to Saima. "Do you think—?"

"Don't know. Really – I haven't a clue." Saima sounded intrigued, and possibly a little miffed, Annabel thought. Josh had completely ignored her, after all.

Katie wandered over, carrying her prompt script. One of the dances had just gone completely pear-shaped and Ms Loftus was trying to sort it out, so she wasn't needed. "What was Josh Matthews talking to you about?"

"Oh, just stuff." Annabel was practically glowing.

"His girlfriend didn't look happy."

Annabel reacted immediately to Katie's tone of voice. "I didn't make him talk to me, Katie! I can't help it if she's jealous – we were chatting about acting, that's all."

"OK, OK! I was just saying. Hey, have you noticed Ms Loftus giving me funny looks today? I haven't made any mistakes with the prompting, but she keeps giving me this kind of thoughtful stare – it's really weird."

Annabel and Saima peered over Katie's shoulder at Ms Loftus, who *did* only seem to have one eye on the dancing and the other on them.

"She's coming over!" Saima squeaked. "What've you done, Katie?"

Nothing, as it turned out. Ms Loftus was smiling hopefully, and she appeared to be a Drama teacher in the throes of a Big Idea.

"Katie and Annabel!" Her smile got bigger, and she seemed to be savouring the names as she said them. "I've been wondering, Annabel, about how we are going to manage your transformation scene. I'd like it to look really good. Mr Hatton's got some great ideas about dry ice and pyrotechnics – stage fireworks, you know – but it suddenly struck me when I saw you two together earlier on that we've got a brilliant opportunity here. If we fiddle with the lines slightly so that you have to go off, Annabel, to get something, perhaps, just before Saima does the spell-song, then *Katie* can come back on wearing another version of your rags costume, while you get changed. Then we use the dry ice and you run on in your ball dress when the stage is covered in smoke – and there we go, instantaneous transformation! What do you think?"

Annabel looked pleadingly at Katie. It would be brilliant!

Katie didn't seem quite so excited. "But I'm prompting!" she protested.

"Oh well, I'm sure Megan can do that bit. can't she? And it's Saima's song, anyway; that won't need prompting, will it Saima?" Ms Loftus beamed at Saima, and didn't wait for an answer. "You'll literally just have to stand there, Katie, that's all, I promise."

"I'm no good at acting, really, Ms Loftus."

"Oh, Katie, it's just standing there wearing the costume, that's all." Annabel grinned. "You know you're good at pretending to be me!"

Katie glared at her. In her opinion, Annabel wasn't nearly grateful enough. It was her that owed Katie a favour right now, not the other way around. She growled, "OK," as mulishly as she felt she could get away with.

Ms Loftus was too excited about her plan to notice that Katie was less than keen. "Fantastic! I'll go and tell Miss Davies we need another set of rags." She dashed off to break the news.

"Thanks, Katie!" Annabel hugged her hard. "This is going to be so cool!"

Ten minutes later, Katie was sitting on the edge of the stage with Megan, still feeling slightly grumpy. It was nearly time to go home, and they were waiting for Becky and Fran and David to come down from the art studio, and for Annabel and Saima who were trying on costumes.

"Are you sure you're OK with this?" asked Megan, who'd been told about the new plan immediately.

Katie wrinkled her nose. "Oh, I suppose so. I don't actually have to do anything. It means I'll be wearing that silly costume all through the first half though, which is a pain."

"Mmmm." Megan nodded sympathetically. "Oh look, there are the others. Just Bel and Saima now."

Becky, Fran and David ran over.

David grinned at Katie. "So you've got a starring role now, then?"

Katie stared at him. "How did you know?"

"Miss Davies came into the studio to moan to Mrs Cranmer about having to make another costume, and we just happened to be close by."

Becky nudged him. "You're such a gossip. You're worse than us."

David just shrugged and smiled in response. "Hey, you two ought to come and see our set – it's going to be really cool."

Fran looked pleased – after all, she had drawn the original design. "Mrs Cranmer's given us loads of gold paint, so it'll really look like a palace. With all the costumes and everything, it's going to look fantastic."

Suddenly their conversation was

interrupted. Furious voices were coming from the other side of the stage.

"I don't believe you! If you don't stop talking to her then I don't want to go out with you any more."

"I'm acting with her – stop being so thick, Julianne." Josh's voice was dripping with contempt.

David frowned. "He's such a scumbag."

Katie and the others looked surprised. "Who, Josh Matthews?"

"Yeah. I know him from football. He treats Julianne really badly, and he thinks he can do what he likes just because he's good-looking. He's always making nasty comments about people as well."

The girls exchanged glances. Katie wondered if David was jealous because Josh was good at football, but he didn't look jealous, just annoyed, and sorry for Julianne. This was a big problem – Annabel really liked Josh, and it sounded like he might not be going out with

Julianne for much longer. Then what would happen? It might be difficult to persuade Annabel he was bad news.

"Are you sure—" Becky was starting to ask anxiously, when suddenly Julianne dashed out and raced past them in tears. She caught sight of Katie and Becky and spat, "This is all your fault! I hate you!" at Becky as she ran off.

Becky looked shocked, and David put his arm round her. "It's OK, she thought you were Bel, that's all."

Katie got up. "Come on. Let's go and wait outside. I don't want to have to talk to him. Let's hope Bel goes off him soon!"

Chapter Nine

"Sorry everybody! Just sit tight for the moment – Mr Hatton's having some trouble with the lighting board."

"Tell me about it," muttered Annabel crossly. The silvery-purple lighting for her transformation scene had come out a sickening green when Mr Hatton ran through the effects earlier on, and since then he and the boys running the lights had been climbing up and down ladders looking harassed.

"I thought it looked good," someone sniggered. "It suited you, Annabel." Amy was standing behind her, wearing her costume.

"Not as much as that make-up suits you. It's a huge improvement, Amy, you should wear it all the time. And I *love* what you've done to your hair."

Amy's costume included a greying wig and a lot of lines on her face, and she was very sensitive about it. She stalked off furiously.

Everyone was getting a bit snappish and short-tempered – they seemed to have been waiting for ages to start the dress rehearsal. It was a good thing that Ms Loftus had warned them to bring snacks in with them, although Miss Davies was running about in a panic pouncing on anyone who looked as though they might be daring to eat in their costume. She had some overall things that anybody who wanted to consume so much as a morsel of chocolate had to put on over the top.

It felt very weird being at school on a Saturday afternoon, Annabel thought. But they couldn't possibly have done this after school – they'd have been there all night. She turned to Saima, who was sitting next to her, about to say something along these lines, but stopped when she caught sight of her friend's face. Saima was looking really pale.

"Are you OK?"

Saima gulped. "Being in our costumes, and having all the sets and lights and everything – it all seems really scary! I don't think I can remember how my song goes!"

"Course you can," Annabel told her firmly. "You know it backwards, Saima, you do it brilliantly. And you look amazing. I'm so jealous of those wings."

Miss Davies had proudly revealed the finishing touch to Saima's costume when they turned up to get ready that afternoon. The wings were made of golden gauzy stuff to match Saima's gold dress. They were attached to her back with straps that were hidden by the dress, and they quivered beautifully whenever she moved.

"I'm just really nervous. I wish we could get on with it! What happens if I freeze up when I'm onstage?"

Amy was suddenly back, flanked by Cara and Emily in their court lady costumes, and all looking superior. "If you think that you're going to mess up you shouldn't have auditioned in the first place. You've got a solo – if you do it wrong you'll spoil everything. It's really selfish of you only to be saying this now, Saima. Somebody else could have had that part, somebody who'd do it properly."

"Somebody like you, I suppose!" retorted Annabel, who could see that Saima, who wouldn't normally have let Amy get away with that sort of thing, had tears in her eyes.

"Well, why not?" Amy snapped back.

"Because Saima's better than you'd ever be, even if she is nervous. She can sing in tune for a start, and she doesn't have all those expensive singing lessons you're always boasting about."

"I have a trained voice—"

"Yeah, trained like a dog, Amy. You sound like a poodle getting a haircut, it's horrible!"

"Right everyone! Places please, we're finally getting under way." Ms Loftus effectively stopped their argument – everyone was desperate to get going. Amy contented herself with glaring at Annabel and Saima, then whisked her heavy brocade skirts round and flounced off.

"C'mon, Saima. It's going to be fine. You're onstage with me most of the time, remember, and we'll cover for each other if anything goes wrong. And there's Katie and Megan prompting too, there's no way they'll let you mess up." Annabel hugged Saima carefully – the fairy wings were pretty fragile.

"Break a leg!" said Saima, summoning up a small smile as they walked to the wings to wait for their entrances. Becky, Fran and David were going to be fetching people in time for their scenes throughout the play, but everyone wanted to watch the beginning rather than waiting in the dressing rooms – it was too exciting!

The scene with Cinderella's parents went perfectly, and then it was Annabel's turn. Her first solo was a sad one, about how lonely she was, and how much she missed her parents who'd died when she was little. Ms Loftus and Mr Becket had told her to aim to have the entire audience sniffing if possible – she had to really pile on the emotion. Luckily Annabel adored being a bit over the top, so she had no problem with this. Having very large blue eyes didn't hurt either. She had to end the song sitting at the edge of the stage with her knees curled up under her, and then collapse to the floor and cry, until the boys playing the Ugly Sisters interrupted her.

Katie, who was sitting in the wings with her prompt script, wearing the hated ragged costume and a huge set of headphones and a little mike so she could talk to the stage crew, rolled her eyes at Becky. Annabel was milking it for all it was worth! She could actually cry on cue, and she wept bitterly and realistically until Joe and Pete came in and started shouting at her. Everyone creased up then – it was very clever of Ms Loftus, Annabel had explained, as the audience went straight from the really sad bit to the comic turn, so the sad bit seemed sadder and the funny bit funnier. Miss Davies had really gone to town on Joe and Pete – they had enormous dresses on with stripy tights underneath, high heels (they'd had to be taught how to walk in them), wigs with loads of feathers and bows in, and amazingly awful make-up.

After her first scene Annabel had a break, so she headed to the dressing room to get a drink of water. Manor Hill was very lucky – the hall was fitted out with a really good stage, with loads of equipment, and proper dressing rooms behind. It was great – it made Annabel feel like a real actress, even if she was sharing the dressing room with about twenty other girls. The dressing room was empty at the moment – everyone was still watching from the wings, she supposed. She slumped into a chair, suddenly feeling tired – she'd been so keyed up all day that as soon as she relaxed it really hit her. The dressing room had a monitor in the corner that showed what was happening onstage and so Annabel knew she had plenty of time. She would need to start psyching herself up again in about five minutes though. She'd do some voice exercises and stretches so as to be on form for her next bit, which was the transformation scene with Saima. She lolled back in the chair, and had just closed her eyes for a second when the dressing-room door slammed open and Amy rushed in. She looked totally weird because she was in her costume and make-up, but didn't have her wig on, so her lined face was topped off with her own wavy strawberry-blonde hair.

"What's up with you?" Annabel asked, in a much more friendly way than she'd normally speak to Amy. She'd been caught on the hop by

Amy's sudden entrance, and Amy looked really upset – Annabel was too nice to be mean to someone who was clearly in a state, even if she did hate her guts.

Amy seemed to have temporarily forgotten their war as well. "I've lost my wig! I took it off because it was making me so hot, and now I can't find it. It's got to be in here somewhere, I've looked everywhere else."

Annabel looked up at the monitor. "Hey, aren't you meant to be on in a minute?"

"*Yes!*" Amy snarled back. "And I can't go on without my wig, Miss Davies'll murder me – it's hired and I'm supposed to take really good care of it. Oh, where *is* it?" She was rifling through piles of clothes as she spoke, desperately searching, and not caring that she was making a total mess that would panic a whole load of other people when they arrived for their next change.

Annabel got up to help. "Be careful – I don't think it'll be in all that stuff. Look, you and

Emily and Cara were sitting over here before, maybe you left it – oh, is that it, under the bench?"

"Yes!" Amy swooped down to retrieve it, then looked up at the monitor and gasped. "Oh no, they're coming off – it's me next!"

Annabel rushed into action as Amy was obviously dithering about whether to get onstage now or stop to put her wig on. "Come on, get into the wings and then I'll put the wig on for you – run!"

They raced for the wings, and Annabel managed to cram Amy into her wig and crown just in time, and then literally shoved her on to the stage for her entrance.

"What was all that about?" whispered Becky in amazement.

"She couldn't find her wig – oh no, look, she's dried."

Amy was standing onstage staring desperately at Josh and the boy playing the king. The panic about her wig had clearly thrown her, and she'd forgotten her lines. She just about remembered them when Katie prompted her, but she flushed scarlet under her makeup and looked furious with herself. The scene limped along as Amy, who wasn't normally a bad actress, never quite recovered herself.

Annabel watched critically. That was the problem with getting prompted – it threw you, and then it was really hard to get back into the character. As Amy came off at the end of the scene she smiled at her – a perfectly nice, natural, sympathetic smile. "Don't worry – it was just because of the wig. You'll be fine for the real thing."

She was expecting Amy to be a bit upset, but to say thank you for helping her out, at least. She didn't. What she actually did was grab Annabel's arm and drag her out of the wings into the dressing-room corridor.

"Hey! I've got to be on in a minute, what are you doing?"

Amy shook her. "This is all your fault!" she hissed. "You did it, didn't you? You hid my wig on purpose to make me late!"

"Ow! Stop it! No, of course I didn't, I found it for you, you saw me!"

"Yes, after you'd hidden it first! I'm not that stupid, Annabel Ryan, why should you suddenly be all nice and helpful like that? You'd set it up, you sneaky—"

"Hey!" Becky, David and Fran had chased after them, and Becky made a grab for Amy's arm. "Stop it!"

David rather gingerly caught Amy's other arm – but Amy shook them off and disappeared down the corridor, apparently in tears.

"Wow! What was all that about?" asked David, looking at Annabel in amazement. "She's really got it in for you!"

"She's crazy," muttered Annabel, massaging her arm. "It's a good thing you lot turned up – she'd have had my dead body buried in the props box any minute. Hey! I've got to be on!" She rushed off, leaving Becky, David and Fran staring after her.

After that little drama, the rest of the dress rehearsal seemed pretty straightforward to Annabel. The only hiccup was when she nearly lost it in the transformation scene. The dry ice and stage fireworks looked fantastic, but the expression on Katie's face as she stood there in the rags costume was so funny. Cinderella was clearly not happy about the whole experience.

Ms Loftus was cautiously optimistic as she called everybody out front for a post-mortem. "Well done, all of you, that was very good. Words though, please – Katie had to do far too much prompting! And that reminds me, I'd just like to say thank you to all the technical crew, they did brilliantly. And to the set-painters, the scenery looks fantastic. Round of applause for all of them, please!"

*

It wasn't until they got home that night that the triplets finally had a chance to talk about what had happened with Amy.

Annabel had almost forgotten about it – everyone had been so nice about her performance that she was practically walking on air. Katie brought her back down to earth with a bump at tea that night.

"Why were you fighting with Amy, Bel?"

Mrs Ryan looked up sharply. "Fighting?"

"I wasn't! She was fighting with me! Honestly, Mum, she's mad. She lost her wig, and I found it for her, and then she messed up her scene because she was in a panic. Then she just went crazy and said it was my fault. She said I'd hidden it."

"Oh, so that's why she messed up that scene," Katie exclaimed. "I did wonder, 'cause she'd never lost it like that before. But honestly, did she really think you'd set it all up? That's stupid."

"I bet she didn't really," Becky said

thoughtfully. "She probably didn't want to admit it was her own fault — she was desperate to find someone else to blame, and you were there. If I were you, Bel, I'd stay well out of her way. . ."

Chapter Ten

"It's true, honestly, I read it somewhere! It's really bad luck to have a good dress rehearsal, it means the performance is going to go totally wrong." Annabel stabbed her fork at Auntie Janet for emphasis, and then put it down. "Oh, I'm too nervous, I can't eat anything."

"Do you *enjoy* panicking, Bel? It seems like it. Just shut up, can't you?" snapped Katie irritably.

Annabel wisely decided not to argue. Katie, she suspected, was actually quite nervous too. She didn't have to do anything except stand there in her ragged costume and hand Saima the rose that Cinderella had been sent to pick from the garden to finish off the spell, but it was the first time she'd done anything like this since the nativity play at infant school. And she hated having to wear the costume – or, as she preferred to call it, "this stupid outfit". Annabel nipped round the table and gave her sister a hug. "You've only got to be on stage for two minutes, and it'll be so easy. You don't need to worry. I'm sorry about being jittery, but I just can't stand the idea that something might go wrong. We've all worked so hard!"

"Yes, it's really nice that all three of you are involved," Auntie Janet smiled round at them. "I'm so looking forward to it. What time do we need to set off? You'll need a while to change, won't you?"

"I'm going to run the girls up to the school any minute, and come back for you, Jan," explained Mrs Ryan. "Otherwise we'll be sitting around for hours, and I know what the chairs are like in that hall."

"Right. OK, Annabel, see you onstage! Break a leg!"

"I can see Mum and Auntie Janet in the audience!" Annabel was peeking through a tiny gap round the side of the curtains. "Urrgh, they're sitting in front of Max and his dad."

"Get back!" Katie hissed. "People will see you!" She was taking her ASM duties very seriously.

"Oh, I wish I was in the first scene, I just want to get on with it," Annabel moaned, but Katie was ignoring her. Her job was about to start.

"Becky, is everyone ready for Scene One?" she asked over the mike. Obviously the answer was yes, as she went on, "OK, house lights down, and go with the curtains!" Annabel dug her nails into her palms – she so wanted everything to go right!

For the first scene she and Saima watched the stage over Katie's shoulder as she sat with the prompt script, and tried to resist fiddling with the stuff on Megan's props table. Annabel grinned to herself as a low murmur of laughter sounded from the hall. The audience seemed to be enjoying it – they were laughing in the right places, and there hadn't been any of those horrible dead pauses where a line fell flat. She seemed to have got past being nervous now, she noticed thankfully. She was just really looking forward to getting onstage – there was just the big crowd scene, where the herald announced to everyone that the prince was to be married, and then it was her!

"Annabel."

Annabel jumped. It was Amy, and Annabel took a step back, wondering if she was about to make another grab for her. "What do you want?" she asked angrily. Saima scowled, and moved closer to back her up, and Katie darted a swift glance at them – she had to concentrate on what was happening on stage, but she was desperate to know what was going on.

Amy put up her hands in a "back off" gesture. "I'm only trying to help!" she said innocently. "I thought you'd want to know, that's all. I just saw your sister – she's really upset."

"Becky? What's the matter with her?" Annabel looked round anxiously, as though expecting to find Becky somewhere.

"She had a row with her boyfriend, um, what's-his-name. . ."

"David?"

"Yeah. Anyway, she was really crying, and she ran off – I think she went to the dressing room. I thought you might want to know."

"Thanks!" Annabel was already halfway out of the wings – if Becky and David had had a fight her sister would be devastated.

"Bel! You can't go!" Saima hissed. "You're on soon!"

"I'll be back!" Annabel whispered. "I will –

148

don't worry!" Saima and Megan were looking worried, and Katie was frantically shaking her head, but Annabel was gone.

Annabel pelted down the corridor. She reckoned she had about three minutes to find Becky, and sort her out – she'd have to take her back to the wings where Katie and Megan could look after her. Where was Fran? She slammed open the dressing-room door. No Becky. But then she wouldn't be obvious, would she, if she was crying? She'd have curled up somewhere to hide. Perhaps the costume cupboard? Annabel raced down to the other end of the long room. "Becky? Becky, are you there? Please come out, I've got to be on stage in, like, two minutes!"

But unless Becky had climbed inside a cardboard box, she wasn't there either. Annabel glanced up at the monitor. It was no good – she had to get back, now. She dashed out of the dressing room – or rather she would have done, if the door hadn't been locked. . .

Back in the wings, Katie, Megan and Saima were gazing in confusion at Becky and David, who looked remarkably unlike people who'd just had a massive row.

"Hi!" Becky whispered. "We've got nothing to do for a bit, so we'd thought we'd come and see how you're doing! Don't worry, Fran's over there if anything needs doing."

Katie stared at her. "Have you two made up?"

"What?" All five of them were now looking equally confused.

"Amy said you'd had a row. . . Oh no!" Katie's mouth dropped open. "Becky, you were right! She's set Annabel up – quick, you've got to go and find her, Amy's trying to make her miss her entrance! Try the dressing rooms! Go!"

*

Annabel rattled frantically at the door handle. What was going on? Had the door slammed shut behind her somehow? No! Of course – Amy. All at once, everything was clear. Oh, how could she have been so stupid? Amy would never do anything to help the triplets out – if she'd seen Becky crying she was more likely to go into fits of laughter than do anything to help. On the monitor, everyone was going off from the crowd scene, and the curtains were coming across for the scene change – she was supposed to be on!

Outside in the corridor, Becky and David had just run headlong into a familiar figure. "Have you seen Annabel?" David demanded. "She's meant to be on!"

Josh sniggered. "Lost her, have you? You're in trouble, mate." Then he seemed to have a change of heart. He looked thoughtful. "Come on! Let's go and look for her."

Josh strode off down the corridor. Becky and David shrugged and followed him. "Where have you looked? Did you check the dressing rooms? Hey! Look, someone's locked this one! Annabel?"

"Let me out! Please, I'm going to miss my scene!" Annabel sounded desperate. She'd tried shouting and banging, but no one had come. All she could do was stare in horror at the monitor – and the empty stage.

Josh unlocked the door. "Did someone lock you in? I can't believe it, that's so bad." His voice had changed, Becky noticed. The hard, jeering tone had gone, and now he was all honeyed sympathy. "Come on, let's get you onstage!" He grabbed her hand and they raced down the corridor, leaving David and Becky staring after them.

"She's never going to believe he's horrible after *that*," Becky pointed out.

"I know – too bad for Annabel. We'd better go back too. I've got a feeling they won't have made it in time."

*

David was right. As Annabel and Josh were running down the passage, Katie had been staring at an empty stage. The curtains had been closed for ages, and the boys on the lights were asking her what was going on over the cans (Mr Hatton had told them that that was the proper name for the headsets).

Saima was peering round the door to the corridor. "I can't see them! Oh, Katie, what are we going to do?"

Megan took the prompt script off Katie. "Look, we've got to do something. You know Annabel's words, Katie, I've heard you testing her loads of times, you know them better than she does. You'll just have to go on for her until she turns up – you're wearing the costume, and everything."

Katie took the headset off slowly. She knew Megan was right, but she *so* didn't want to do this! She'd been worried enough about just standing on the stage, now she had to talk as well! Megan grabbed the headset and spoke into it. "We're ready – go with the curtains!" She grabbed a sweeping brush and thrust it into Katie's hands. "Go!"

Katie gave her a horrified look, and stepped out on to the stage – by the time the curtains were open she had to be onstage and sweeping the floor.

The curtains rattled open, and there was a sea of faces in front of her. Katie hurriedly looked down again, and decided that Cinderella had better concentrate very hard on the floor. She took a deep breath, and spoke Annabel's first line.

"I'm so tired – I'll never get all this done today, and then I'll be in such trouble." She sniffed miserably, as she'd watched Annabel do. This was OK, just about. She might not be any good, but at least *someone* was on the stage! She carried on, and she was three lines into the next speech when she realized something awful – it was at the end of this speech that Annabel had to sing her solo! Katie stopped dead, then gulped, and carried on *very* slowly. This speech had to last, as there was no way she could do the song. Where on earth was her stupid brainless dim idiot of a sister?

"Katie!" A quiet but panicky hiss was coming from stage left. Megan and – thank goodness! – Annabel were waving at her. "Sweep this way!"

Katie started sweeping furiously – she was within a sentence of the song by now! She whisked the broom over to the side of the stage, and used the duster sticking out of the pocket of her costume to dust the curtains. Then she ducked quickly offstage, and Annabel grabbed the broom. "You're such a star, thank you!"

"And I'm going to kill *you* – get out there!"

Watching from the front, Mrs Ryan looked confused. She'd thought during Annabel's first speech that she must have a bit of stage fright – she didn't look quite right, and her stage presence seemed to have gone. But now

155

she had the audience positively eating out of her hand with the song. The triplets' mum could have sworn that that had been *Katie* at first. . . Just what was going on? At the interval, she tackled her sister.

"So, what do you think?"

"She's excellent – do you think she was nervous at the beginning though? I mean, she did fine, but for the first five minutes, she just didn't have the same sparkle," said Auntie Janet.

Mrs Ryan nodded furiously – she was glad she wasn't imagining things.

"Excuse me – it's Sue Ryan, isn't it?"

Mrs Ryan turned round in surprise. A tall good-looking man was standing there, with a sulky-faced boy beside him. "Jeff Cooper. We spoke on the phone a while ago? This is Max."

Mrs Ryan smiled. "Oh hello. How did you know who I was?"

"Your daughter's name is in the programme – you look so like her. She's really good, isn't she? You must be very proud of her."

Max snarled something, and his father glared at him.

Auntie Jan looked on, intrigued, and put in the odd comment, while the triplets' mum and Max's dad chatted, and Max scowled at the floor. By the time the bell went for the end of the interval she was desperate to find out just who this nice man was, but Mrs Ryan just shushed her. "They're starting again, Jan, stop chatting!"

Annabel's performance got even better in the second half. By the time she was in her ballgown – Mrs Ryan and Auntie Jan nudged each other proudly, it looked so fab! – she looked like she really was wearing an enchanted dress and dancing with the love of her life. Of course, it did help that she was dancing with Josh, who'd not only rescued her earlier on, but had just confided to her at the interval that he and Julianne had split up. Somehow,

Annabel had had difficulty looking properly sympathetic. If only their stage kiss was for real! She was on a high. She really felt like a star, and everyone was treating her like one. Even Mr Hatton had congratulated her in the interval!

Amy's plan had totally backfired – no one seemed to have minded the switch they'd had to do (luckily Ms Loftus hadn't noticed), and the play was going brilliantly. Practically the whole cast had seen what had happened, and the triplets had lost no time explaining the trick Amy had tried to pull. Everyone was disgusted with her, and Amy was stalking around with her nose in the air pretending she didn't care what they were saying.

The second half seemed to fly by. Katie managed not to make Cinderella look as though she was about to be executed in the transformation scene this time, thank goodness. Annabel wished it would slow down, somehow – it almost didn't feel like she'd had time to enjoy it properly! It seemed no time at all before she was holding Josh's hand as they waited for the curtain call – they had to bow together, but he didn't actually need to be holding her hand yet, so that had to be a good sign, didn't it? Annabel listened smugly to the thunderous applause, and glanced over her shoulder at Katie and Becky. To be perfectly honest, they both looked relieved that the evening was nearly over. Annabel grinned back at her sisters as she ran out on to the stage for the last time. She was a star!

"Just never, ever make me do anything like that again!" Katie shoved half a slice of chocolate cake into her mouth in a very expressive fashion and glared at Annabel.

"It wasn't me! I didn't want you doing my favourite scene!" Annabel sounded indignant.

"That's not your favourite, your favourite's when you kiss *Josh*," giggled Saima.

The triplets were sitting in their kitchen

with Fran, Saima, Megan and David, tucking into a gorgeous chocolate cake that Mum had whipped out when they got home. A couple of days before, Annabel had begged to have everyone back after the play – she knew how flat she would feel when it was all over, and a party would definitely help!

Katie leant over the table and whispered to Annabel – Mum and Auntie Janet were in the next room, and Mum still didn't know about Annabel's detention – "That's the second time I've had to be you recently, and I don't like it!"

Annabel grinned. "You should be grateful – it isn't often you get to be someone as lovely as me." Then she ducked, as Katie threatened to throw the rest of her cake at her.

"Hey, if you don't *want* that. . ." David made a grab for it.

"Uh-uh." Katie dodged, and quickly bolted the other half.

Annabel pushed the rest of the cake towards him. "You can have some more though. And it's time to swap presents. You're going to love yours!" She grinned at David, remembering the poster Becky had got him, and then looked round the table at all their friends. Maybe the play *was* finished, but it had been brilliant, and now there was Christmas to look forward to. She got up and grabbed the pile of presents that was sitting temptingly on the kitchen counter. "Come on, let's open them! Happy Christmas, you lot!"

Look out for more

Look out for

Look out for

HOLLY WEBB

EMILY FEATHER
and the Enchanted Door

HOLLY WEBB

EMILY FEATHER
and the Secret Mirror

HOLLY WEBB

EMILY FEATHER
and the Chest of Charms

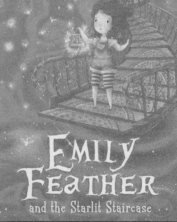

HOLLY WEBB

EMILY FEATHER
and the Starlit Staircase

HOLLY has always loved animals.
As a child, she had two dogs, a cat, and at
one point, nine gerbils (an accident).
Holly's other love is books. Holly now lives
in Reading with her husband, three sons
and a very spoilt cat.